CRENSHAW

KATHERINE APPLEGATE

Crenshaw

FEIWEL AND FRIENDS

NEW YORK

A FEIWEL AND FRIENDS BOOK
An Imprint of Macmillan

Library of Congress Cataloging-in-Publication Data is available.

ISBN 978-1-250-04323-8 (hardcover) / ISBN 978-1-250-08022-6 (ebook)

Book design by Liz Dresner

Feiwel and Friends logo designed by Filomena Tuosto

First Edition—2015

10 9 8 7 6 5 4 3 2 1

mackids.com

for Jake

Dr. Sanderson:

"Think carefully, Dowd. Didn't you know somebody, sometime, someplace by the name of Harvey? Didn't you ever know anybody by that name?"

Elwood P. Dowd:

"No, no, not one, Doctor. Maybe that's why I always had such hopes for it."

—MARY CHASE, *Harvey* (1944)

PART ONE

A door is to open

—A HOLE IS TO DIG:

A FIRST BOOK OF FIRST DEFINITIONS,

written by Ruth Krauss and

illustrated by Maurice Sendak

1

I noticed several weird things about the surfboarding cat.

Thing number one: He was a surfboarding cat.

Thing number two: He was wearing a T-shirt. It said CATS RULE, DOGS DROOL.

Thing number three: He was holding a closed umbrella, like he was worried about getting wet. Which, when you think about it, is kind of *not* the point of surfing.

Thing number four: No one else on the beach seemed to see him.

He'd grabbed a good wave, and his ride was smooth. But as the cat neared shore, he made the mistake of opening his umbrella. A gust of wind yanked him into the sky. He missed a seagull by seconds.

Even the gull didn't seem to notice him.

The cat floated over me like a furry balloon. I looked straight up. He looked straight down. He waved.

His coat was black and white, penguin style. He looked like he was heading somewhere fancy in a hairy tuxedo.

He also looked awfully familiar.

"Crenshaw," I whispered.

I glanced around me. I saw sand-castle builders and Frisbee tossers and crab chasers. But I didn't see anyone looking at the floating, umbrella-toting surfer cat in the sky.

I squeezed my eyes shut and counted to ten. Slowly.

Ten seconds seemed like the right amount of time for me to stop being crazy.

I felt a little dizzy. But that happens sometimes when I'm hungry. I hadn't eaten since breakfast.

When I opened my eyes, I sighed with relief. The cat was gone. The sky was endless and empty.

Whap. Inches from my toes, the umbrella landed in the sand like a giant dart.

It was red and yellow plastic, decorated with pictures of tiny smiling mice. On the handle, printed in crayon, were the words THIS BUMBERSHOOT BELONGS TO CRENSHAW.

I closed my eyes again. I counted to ten. I opened my eyes, and the umbrella—or the bumbershoot, or whatever it was—had vanished. Just like the cat.

It was late June, nice and warm, but I shivered.

I felt the way you do the instant before you leap into the deep end of a pool.

You're on your way to somewhere else. You're not there yet. But you know there's no turning back.

2

Here's the thing: I am not an imaginary friend kind of guy.

Seriously. This fall I go into fifth grade. At my age, it's not good to have a reputation for being crazy.

I like facts. Always have. True stuff. Two-plus-two-equals-four facts. Brussels-sprouts-taste-like-dirty-gym-socks facts.

Okay, maybe that second one's just an opinion. And anyway, I've never eaten a dirty gym sock so I could be wrong.

Facts are important to scientists, which is what I want to be when I grow up. Nature facts are my favorite kind. Especially the ones that make people say *No way.*

Like the fact that a cheetah can run seventy miles per hour.

Or the fact that a headless cockroach can survive for more than two weeks.

Or the fact that when a horned toad gets mad it shoots blood from its eyes.

I want to be an animal scientist. I'm not sure what kind. Right now I really like bats. I also like cheetahs and cats and dogs and snakes and rats and manatees. So those are some options.

I like dinosaurs, too, except for them all being dead. For a while, my friend Marisol and I both wanted to be paleontologists and search for dinosaur fossils. She used to bury chicken bone leftovers in her sandbox for digging practice.

Marisol and I started a dog-walking service this summer. It's called See Spot Walk. Sometimes when we're walking dogs, we'll trade nature facts. Yesterday she told me that a bat can eat 1,200 mosquitoes in an hour.

Facts are so much better than stories. You can't see a story. You can't hold it in your hand and measure it.

You can't hold a manatee in your hand either. But still. Stories are lies, when you get right down to it. And I don't like being lied to.

I've never been much into make-believe stuff. When I was a kid, I didn't dress up like Batman or talk to stuffed animals or worry about monsters under my bed.

My parents say, when I was in pre-K, I marched around telling everybody I was the mayor of Earth. But that was just for a couple of days.

Sure, I had my Crenshaw phase. But lots of kids have an imaginary friend.

Once my parents took me to see the Easter Bunny at the mall. We stood on fake grass next to a giant fake egg in a giant fake basket. When it was my turn to pose with the bunny, I took one look at his paw and yanked it right off.

A man's hand was inside. It had a gold wedding ring and tufts of blondish hair.

"This man is not a rabbit!" I shouted. A little girl started bawling.

The mall manager made us leave. I did not get the free basket with candy eggs or a photo with the fake rabbit.

That was the first time I realized people don't always like to hear the truth.

3

After the Easter Bunny incident, my parents started to worry.

Except for my two days as mayor of Earth, I didn't seem to have much of an imagination. They thought maybe I was too grown-up. Too serious.

My dad wondered if he should have read me more fairy tales.

My mom wondered if she should have let me watch so many nature shows where animals eat each other.

They asked my grandma for advice. They wanted to know if I was acting too adult for my age.

She said not to worry.

No matter how adult I seemed, she told them, I would definitely grow out of it when I became a teenager.

4

A few hours after my Crenshaw sighting at the beach, he appeared again.

No surfboard this time. No umbrella.

No body, either.

Still. I knew he was there.

It was about six in the evening. My sister, Robin, and I were playing cerealball in the living room of our apartment. Cerealball is a good trick for when you're hungry and there's nothing much to eat till morning. We invented it when our stomachs were grumbling to each other. *Wow, I would love a piece of pepperoni pizza,* my stomach would growl. And then hers would grumble, *Yeah, or maybe a Ritz cracker with peanut butter.*

Robin loves Ritzes.

Cerealball is easy to play. All you need are a few Cheerios or even a little piece of bread all torn up. M&M's would be good too, if your mom isn't around to say no sugar. But unless it's right after Halloween you probably don't have any.

In my family those guys go really fast.

First you pick a target to throw at. A bowl or cup works fine. Don't use a wastebasket, because that might have germs. Sometimes I use Robin's T-ball cap. Although that's probably pretty gross, too.

For a five-year-old, that girl can really sweat.

What you do is throw your one piece of cereal and try to make a basket. The rule is you can't eat that piece until you score. Make sure your target's far away or you'll finish your food too fast.

The trick is that you take so long to hit the target, you forget about being hungry. For a while, anyway.

I like to use Cheerios and Robin likes Frosted Flakes. But you can't be picky when the cupboard is bare. My mom says that sometimes.

If you run out of cereal and your stomach's still growling, you can always try chewing a piece of gum to distract yourself. Stuck behind your ear is a good hiding place if you want to use your gum again. Even if the flavor is gone your teeth get a workout.

Crenshaw showed up—at least he *seemed* to show up—while we were busy throwing my dad's bran cereal into Robin's cap. It was my turn to throw, and I got a direct hit. When I went to take out the cereal piece, I found four purple jelly beans instead.

I love purple jelly beans.

I stared a long time at those things. "Where did the jelly beans come from?" I finally asked.

Robin grabbed the cap. I started to pull it away, but then I changed my mind. Robin is small, but you don't want to mess with her.

She bites.

"It's magic!" she said. She started dividing up the jelly beans. "One for me, one for you, two for me—"

"Seriously, Robin. Stop kidding around. Where?"

Robin gobbled down two jelly beans. "Shlp tchzzzn muh," she said, which I figured meant "stop teasing me" in candy-mouth.

Aretha, our big Labrador mutt, rushed over to check things out. "No candy for you," Robin said. "You are a dog so you eat dog food, young lady."

But Aretha didn't seem interested in the candy. She was sniffing the air, ears cocked toward the front door, as if we had a guest approaching.

"Mom," I yelled, "did you buy some jelly beans?"

"Sure," she called back from the kitchen. "They're to go with the caviar."

"I'm serious," I said, picking up my two pieces.

"Just eat Dad's cereal, Jackson. You'll poop for a week," she answered.

A second later she appeared in the doorway, a dish towel in her hands. "Are you guys still hungry?" She sighed. "I've got a little mac and cheese left over from dinner. And there's half an apple you could share."

"I'm fine," I said quickly. Back in the old days, when we always had food in the house, I would whine if we were out of my favorite stuff. But lately we'd been running out of everything, and I had the feeling my parents felt lousy about it.

"We have jelly beans, Mom," Robin said.

"Well, okay, then. As long as you're eating something nutritious," said my mom. "I get my paycheck at Rite Aid tomorrow, and I'll stop by the grocery store and pick up some food after work."

She gave a little nod, like she'd checked something off a list, and went back to the kitchen.

"Aren't you gonna eat your jelly beans?" Robin asked me, twirling her yellow ponytail around her finger. "Because if you want me to do you a big favor I guess I could eat them for you."

"I'm going to eat them," I said. "Just not . . . yet."

"Why not? They're purple. Your favorite."

"I need to think about them first."

17

"You are a weirdo brother," said Robin. "I'm going to my room. Aretha wants to play dress-up."

"I doubt that," I said. I held a jelly bean up to the light. It looked harmless enough.

"She especially likes hats and also socks," Robin said as she left with the dog. "Don't you, baby?"

Aretha's tail wagged. She was always up for anything. But as she left with Robin, she glanced over her shoulder at the front window and whined.

I went to the window and peered outside. I checked behind the couch. I flung open the hall closet.

Nothing. Nobody.

No surfing cats. No Crenshaw.

I hadn't told anybody about what I'd seen at the beach. Robin would just think I was messing with her. My mom and dad would do one of two things. Either they'd freak out and worry I was going crazy. Or they'd think it was adorable that I was pretending to hang out with my old invisible friend.

I sniffed the jelly beans. They smelled not-quite-grapey, in a good way. They looked real. They felt real. And my real little sister had just eaten some.

Rule number one for scientists is this: There is always a logical explanation for things. I just had to figure out what it was.

Maybe the jelly beans weren't real, and I was just tired or sick. Delirious, even.

I checked my forehead. Unfortunately, I did not seem to have a fever.

Maybe I'd gotten sunstroke at the beach. I wasn't exactly sure what sunstroke was, but it sounded like something that might make you see flying cats and magic jelly beans.

Maybe I was asleep, stuck in the middle of a long, weird, totally annoying dream.

Still. Didn't the jelly beans in my hand seem extremely real?

Maybe I was just hungry. Hunger can make you feel pretty weird. Even pretty crazy.

I ate my first jelly bean slowly and carefully. If you take tiny bites, your food lasts longer.

A voice in my head said, *Never take candy from strangers.* But Robin had survived. And if there was a stranger involved, he was an invisible one.

There had to be a logical explanation. But for now, the only thing I knew for sure was that purple jelly beans tasted way better than bran cereal.

5

The first time I met Crenshaw was about three years ago, right after first grade ended.

It was early evening, and my family and I had parked at a rest stop off a highway. I was lying on the grass near a picnic table, gazing up at the stars blinking to life.

I heard a noise, a wheels-on-gravel skateboard sound. I sat up on my elbows. Sure enough, a skater on a board was threading his way through the parking lot.

I could see right away that he was an unusual guy.

He was a black and white kitten. A big one, taller than me. His eyes were the sparkly color of morning grass. He was wearing a black and orange San Francisco Giants baseball cap.

He hopped off his board and headed my way. He was standing on two legs just like a human.

"Meow," he said.

"Meow," I said back, because it seemed polite.

He leaned close and sniffed my hair. "Do you have any purple jelly beans?"

I jumped to my feet. It was his lucky day. I just happened to have two purple jelly beans in my jeans pocket.

They were a little smushed, but we each ate one anyway.

I told the cat my name was Jackson.

He said yes, of course it is.

I asked him what his name was.

He asked what did I want his name to be.

It was a surprising question. But I had already figured out he was a surprising guy.

I thought for a while. It was a big decision. People care a lot about names.

Finally I said, "Crenshaw would be a good name for a cat, I think."

He didn't smile because cats don't smile.

But I could tell he was pleased.

"Crenshaw it is," he said.

6

I don't know where I got the name Crenshaw.

No one in my family has ever known a Crenshaw.

We don't have any Crenshaw relatives or Crenshaw friends or Crenshaw teachers.

I'd never been to Crenshaw, Mississippi, or Crenshaw, Pennsylvania, or Crenshaw Boulevard in Los Angeles.

I'd never read a book about a Crenshaw or seen a TV show with a Crenshaw in it.

Somehow Crenshaw just seemed right.

Everybody in my family was named after somebody or something else. My dad was named after his grandpa. My mom was named after her aunt. My sister and I weren't even named after people. We were named after guitars.

I was named after my dad's guitar. It was designed by a manufacturer called Jackson. My sister was named after the company that made my mom's guitar.

My parents used to be musicians. Starving musicians is what my mom calls it. After I was born, they stopped being musicians and became normal people. Since they'd run out of instruments, my parents named our dog after a famous singer called Aretha Franklin. That was after Robin wanted to name her Fairy Princess Cutie Pie and I wanted to call her Dog.

At least our middle names came from people and not instruments. Orson and Marybelle were my dad's uncle and my mom's great-grandma. Those folks are dead, so I don't know if they're good names or not.

Dad says his uncle was a charming curmudgeon,

which I think means grumpy with some niceness thrown in.

Honestly, another middle name might have been better. A brand-new one. One that wasn't already used up.

Maybe that's why I liked the name Crenshaw. It felt like a blank piece of paper before you draw on it.

It was an anything-is-possible kind of name.

7

I don't exactly remember how I felt about Crenshaw that day we met.

It was a long time ago.

I don't remember lots of stuff about what happened when I was young.

I don't remember being born. Or learning to walk. Or wearing diapers. Which is probably not something you want to remember anyway.

Memory is weird. I remember getting lost at the

grocery store when I was four. But I don't remember getting found by my mom and dad, who were yelling and crying at the same time. I only know that part because they told me about it.

I remember when my little sister first came home. But I don't remember trying to put her in a box so we could mail her back to the hospital.

My parents enjoy telling people that story.

I'm not even sure why Crenshaw was a cat, and not a dog or an alligator or a Tyrannosaurus rex with three heads.

When I try to remember my whole entire life, it feels like a Lego project where you're missing some of the important pieces, like a robot mini-figure or a monster-truck wheel. You do the best you can to put things together, but you know it's not quite like the picture on the box.

It seems like I should have thought to myself, Wow, a cat is talking to me, and that is not something that usually happens at a highway rest stop.

But all I remember thinking is how great it was to have a friend who liked purple jelly beans as much as I did.

8

A couple of hours after the mysterious jelly bean appearance during cerealball, my mom gave Robin and me each a grocery bag. She said they were for our keepsakes. A bunch of our things were going to be sold at a yard sale on Sunday, except for important stuff like shoes and mattresses and a few dishes. My parents were hoping to make enough money to pay some back rent and maybe the water bill, too.

Robin asked what is a keepsake. My mom said it's an object you treasure. Then she said things don't really matter, as long as we have each other.

I asked what were her keepsakes and my dad's. She said probably their guitars would be at the top of the list, and maybe books, because those were always important.

Robin said she would bring her Lyle book for sure.

My sister's favorite book in the world is *The House on East 88th Street*. It's about a crocodile named Lyle who lives with a family. Lyle likes to hang out in the bathtub and walk the dog.

Robin knows every word of that book by heart.

Later, at bedtime, my dad read the Lyle book to Robin. I stood at her bedroom door and listened to him reading. He and my mom and Robin and Aretha were all squished on her mattress. It was on the floor. The wooden parts were going to be sold.

"Come join us, Jackson," my mom said. "There's lots of room."

My dad is tall and so is my mom and Robin's mattress is tiny. There wasn't any room.

"I'm good," I said.

Looking at my family, all there together, I felt like a relative from out of town. Like I belonged to them, but not as much as they belonged to each other. Partly that was because they look so much alike, blond and gray-eyed and cheerful. My hair and eyes are darker, and sometimes so is my mood.

Emptied out, it didn't look like Robin's room anymore. Except for her pink lamp. And the marks on the wall that showed how much she had grown. And the red spot on the carpet where she'd spilled cranberry-apple juice. Robin was practicing her T-ball batting and she got a little carried away.

"SWISH, SWASH, SPLASH, SPLOOSH . . ." read my dad.

"Not sploosh, Daddy," Robin said.

"Smoosh? Splish? Swash?"

"Stop being silly," she said. She poked him in the chest. "It's 'swoosh'! 'Swoosh,' I tell you!"

I said that I did not think a crocodile would enjoy taking a bath. I'd just read a whole library book about reptiles.

My dad told me to go with the flow.

"Did you know that you can hold a crocodile's jaws closed with a rubber band?" I asked.

My dad smiled. "I wouldn't want to have been the first person who tested that theory."

Robin asked my mom if I had a favorite book when I was little. She didn't ask me, because she was pouting about my bathtub comment.

My mom said, "Jackson really liked *A Hole Is To Dig*. Remember that book, Jackson? We must've read that to you a million times."

"That's more like a dictionary than a made-up story," I said.

" 'A brother is to help you,' " my mom said. Which was a line from the book.

"A brother is to bug you," said Robin. Which was *not* a line from the book.

"A sister is to drive you slowly insane," I replied.

The sun was beginning to set. The sky was tiger-colored, with stripes of black clouds.

"I have to get my stuff ready for the yard sale," I said.

"Hey, stick around, dude," said my dad. "I'll read *A Hole Is To Dig*. Assuming we can find it, that is."

"I'm way too old for that book," I said, even though it was the first thing I'd put in my keepsakes bag.

"Lyle one more time," Robin said. "Pleaseplease pleasepleaseplease?"

"Dad," I asked, "did you buy some purple jelly beans?"

"Nope."

"Then where did they come from? The ones in Robin's T-ball cap? It doesn't make any sense."

"Robin went to Kylie's birthday party yesterday," said my mom. "Did you get them there, sweet pea?"

"Nope," Robin said. "Kylie hates jelly beans. And anyway, I told you they were magic, Jackson."

"There's no such thing as magic," I said.

"Music is magic," said my mom.

"Love is magic," said my dad.

"Rabbits in a hat are magic," said Robin.

"I would put Krispy Kreme doughnuts in the magic category," said my dad.

"How about the smell of a new baby?" asked my mom.

"Kitties are magic!" Robin yelled.

"Indeed," said my dad, scratching Aretha's ear. "And don't forget dogs."

They were still going at it when I shut the door.

9

I love my mom and my dad and usually my sister. But lately they'd really been getting on my nerves.

Robin was a little kid, so of course she was annoying. She'd say things like "What if a dog and a bird got married, Jackson?" Or sing "Wheels on the Bus" three thousand times in a row. Or steal my skateboard and use it for a doll ambulance. The usual little sister stuff.

My parents were more complicated. It's hard to

explain, especially since I know this sounds like a good thing, but they were always looking on the bright side. Even when things were bad—and they'd been bad a lot—they joked. They acted silly. They pretended everything was fine.

Sometimes I just wanted to be treated like a grown-up. I wanted to hear the truth, even if it wasn't a happy truth. I understood things. I knew way more than they thought I did.

But my parents were optimists. They looked at half a glass of water and figured it was half full, not half empty.

Not me. Scientists can't afford to be optimists or pessimists. They just observe the world and see what is. They look at a glass of water and measure 3.75 ounces or whatever, and that's the end of the discussion.

Take my dad. When I was younger, he got sick, really sick. He found out he has this disease called multiple sclerosis. Mostly he has good days, but sometimes he has bad ones when it's hard to walk and he has to use a cane.

When he learned he had MS, my dad acted like it was no big deal, even though he had to quit his job, which was building houses. He said he was tired of listening to hammering all day long. He said he wanted to wear fancy shoes instead of muddy ones, and then he wrote a song about it called "The Muddy Shoes Blues." He said he might work from home, so he taped a sign on the bathroom door that said OFFICE OF MR. THOMAS WADE. My mom put a sign next to it that said I'D RATHER BE FISHING.

And that was that.

Sometimes I just want to ask my parents if my dad is going to be okay or why we don't always have enough food in the house or why they've been arguing so much.

Also, why I couldn't have been an only child.

But I don't ask. Not anymore.

Last fall we were at a neighborhood potluck dinner when Aretha ate a baby's disposable diaper. She had to spend two nights at the vet's until she pooped it out.

"Poop in, poop out," my dad said when we picked her up. "It's the cycle of life."

"The cycle of life is expensive," my mom said, staring at the bill. "Looks like rent's going to be late again this month."

When we got to the car, I came right out and asked if we had enough money for stuff. My dad said not to worry. That we just were a little financially challenged. He said sometimes it's hard to plan for everything, unless you have a crystal ball and can see the future, and if I knew someone with a crystal ball, he would love to borrow it.

My mom said something about winning the lottery, and my dad said if they won the lottery, could he please get a Ferrari, and she said how about a Jaguar, and then I could tell they wanted to change the subject.

I didn't ask any more hard questions after that.

Somehow I just knew my parents didn't want to give me hard answers.

10

After I got ready for bed, I lay on my mattress and thought things over.

I thought about the stuff I'd put in my keepsakes bag. Some photos. A spelling bee trophy. A bunch of nature books. My teddy bear. A clay statue of Crenshaw that I'd made when I was in second grade. My worn-out copy of *A Hole Is To Dig*.

I thought about Crenshaw and the surfboard.

I thought about the purple jelly beans.

Mostly, though, I thought about the signs I'd been noticing.

I am very observant, which is a useful thing for a scientist to be. Here's what I'd been observing:

Big piles of bills.

Parents whispering.

Parents arguing.

Stuff getting sold, like the silver teapot my grandma gave my mom and our laptop computer.

The power going off for two days because we hadn't paid the bill.

Not much food except peanut butter and mac and cheese and Cup O Noodles.

My mom digging under the couch cushions for quarters.

My dad digging under the couch cushions for dimes.

My mom borrowing toilet paper rolls from work.

The landlord coming over and saying "I'm sorry" and shaking his head a lot.

It didn't make sense. My mom had three part-time

jobs. My dad had two part-time jobs. You'd think that would add up to two whole actual jobs, but it didn't seem to.

My mom used to teach music at a middle school until they cut her job. Now she worked as a waitress at two restaurants and as a cashier at a drugstore. She wanted to get another job teaching music, but so far nothing had come up.

After my dad had to quit construction work, he started a handyman business. He did small fix-it stuff, but sometimes he wasn't feeling well and had to cancel appointments. He also gave private guitar lessons. And he was hoping to go to community college part-time to learn computer programming.

I figured my parents had a plan for making everything okay, because parents always have a plan. But when I asked them what it was, they said stuff like maybe they could plant a money tree in the backyard. Or maybe they could start their rock band up again and win a Grammy Award.

I didn't want to leave our apartment, but I could

feel it coming, even if nobody said anything. I knew how things worked. I'd been through this before.

It was too bad, because I really liked where we lived, even though we'd only been there a couple of years. Swanlake Village was the name of our neighborhood. It didn't have any real swans. But all the mailboxes had swans on them, and the community pool had a swan painted on the bottom.

The pool water was always warm. Mom said it was from the sun, but I suspected illegal peeing.

All the streets in Swanlake Village had two words in their names. Ours was Quiet Moon. But there were others, like Sleepy Dove and Weeping Wood and Sunny Glen. My school, Swanlake Elementary, was only two blocks from my house. It didn't have anything with swans on it.

Swanlake Village wasn't a fancy place at all, just a regular old neighborhood. But it was friendly. It was the kind of place where you could smell hot dogs and burgers grilling every weekend. Where kids rode their scooters on the sidewalk and sold lousy lemonade for a quarter a cup. It was a place where you had friends you could count on, like Marisol.

You wouldn't have thought it was a place where people were worried or hungry or sad.

Our school librarian likes to say you can't judge a book by its cover. Maybe it's the same way with neighborhoods. Maybe you can't judge a place by its swans.

11

I finally fell asleep, but around eleven I woke. I got up to go to the bathroom, and as I headed down the hall, I realized my parents were still awake. I could hear them talking in the living room.

They were thinking of places we could go if we couldn't pay the rent.

If I don't become an animal scientist, I would make a great spy.

My mom said how about Gladys and Joe, my

dad's parents. They live in an apartment in New Jersey. My dad said they only had one extra bedroom. Then he declared, "Plus, I couldn't live under his roof. He's the most pigheaded man on the planet."

"Second-most pigheaded," said my mom. "We could try borrowing money from our families."

My dad rubbed his eyes. "Do we have a rich relative I've never met?"

"I see your point," said my mom. Then she said how about my dad's cousin in Idaho who has a ranch, or her mom in Sarasota, who has a condo, or his old buddy Cal, who lives in Maine in a trailer.

My dad asked which of those people would take in two adults, two children, and a dog who eats furniture. Besides, he said, he didn't want to accept anyone's handouts.

"You do realize we can't live in the minivan again," my mom said.

"No," said my dad. "We can't."

"Aretha's a lot bigger. She'd take up the whole middle seat."

"Plus she farts a lot." My dad sighed. "Who knows? Sunday at the yard sale somebody might give us a million bucks for Robin's old high chair."

"Good point," said my mom. "It comes with extra Cheerios stuck to the seat."

They fell silent.

"We should sell the TV," my mom said after a while. "I know it's ancient, but still."

My dad shook his head. "We're not barbarians." He clicked the remote and an old black-and-white movie came to life.

My mom stood. "I'm so tired." She looked at my dad with her arms crossed over her chest. "Look," she said. "There's nothing—nothing at all—wrong with asking for help, Tom."

Her voice was low and slow. It was the voice she used when a fight was coming. My chest tightened. The air felt thick.

"There's everything wrong with asking for help," my dad snapped. "It means we've failed." His voice had changed, too. It was sharp and hard.

"We have *not* failed. We are doing the best we can." My mom gave a frustrated groan. "Life is what happens to you while you're busy making other plans, Tom."

"Really?" My dad was yelling. "So now we're resorting to fortune cookie wisdom? Like that's going to help put food in our kids' mouths?"

"Well, refusing to ask for help isn't going to."

"We *have* asked for help, Sara. We've been to that food pantry more times than I care to admit. But in the end, this is my—our—problem to solve," my dad shouted.

"You're not responsible for getting sick, Tom. And you're not responsible for my getting laid off." My mom threw her hands in the air. "Oh, what's the point? I'm going to bed."

I slipped into the bathroom as my mom stormed

down the hall. She slammed her bedroom door so loudly the whole house seemed to tremble.

I waited a few minutes to be sure the coast was clear. When I headed back to my room, my dad was still on the couch, staring at the gray ghosts moving across the screen.

12

I didn't sleep much after that. I tossed and turned, and finally I got up to get some water. Everyone was asleep. The bathroom door was closed, but light was sneaking out of the cracks.

I heard humming.

I heard splashing.

"Mom?" I said softly. "Dad?"

No answer.

"Robin?"

No answer. More humming.

It sounded like "How Much Is That Doggy in the Window?" but I couldn't be sure.

I thought about whether it might be an ax murderer. But taking a bath didn't seem like an ax murderer kind of thing to do.

I didn't want to open the door.

I opened the door an inch.

More splashing. A sudsy blob floated by.

I opened the door all the way.

Crenshaw was taking a bubble bath.

13

I looked at him. He looked at me.

I flew into the bathroom, shut the door, and locked it.

"Meow," he said. It sounded like a question.

I did not say "meow" back. I did not say anything.

I closed my eyes and counted to ten.

He was still there when I opened them.

Crenshaw seemed even bigger up close. His white

stomach rose from the bubbles like a snowy island. His enormous tail draped over the side of the tub.

"Do you have any purple jelly beans?" he asked. He had thick whiskers that poked out from his face like uncooked spaghetti.

"No." I said it more to myself than to him.

Aretha scratched at the door.

"Not now, girl," I said.

She whined.

Crenshaw wrinkled his nose. "I smell dog."

He was holding one of Robin's rubber duckies. He looked at the duck carefully, then rubbed his forehead on it. Cats have scent glands by their ears, and when they rub on something, it's like writing, in big letters, *THIS IS MINE*.

"You are imaginary," I said in my firmest voice. "You are not real." Crenshaw made himself a beard out of bubbles.

"I invented you when I was seven," I said, "and that means I can un-invent you now."

Crenshaw didn't seem to be paying attention. "If

you don't have purple jelly beans," he said, "red will do in a pinch."

I looked in the mirror. My face was pale and sweaty. I could still see Crenshaw's reflection. He was making a tiny bubble beard for the rubber duck.

"You do not exist," I said to the cat in the mirror.

"I beg to differ," said Crenshaw.

Aretha scratched again. "Fine," I muttered. I eased open the door an inch to make sure no one was in the hallway listening.

Listening to me talk to an imaginary cat.

Aretha bulldozed through like I had a giant, juicy steak waiting in the tub. I locked the door again.

Once she was inside, Aretha stood perfectly still on the bath rug, except for her tail. That was fluttering like a windy-day flag.

"I am positively flummoxed as to why your family felt the need for a dog," said Crenshaw, eyeing her suspiciously. "Why not a cat? An animal with some panache? Some pizzazz? Some dignity?"

"Both my parents are allergic to cats," I said.

I am talking to my imaginary friend.
I invented him when I was seven.
He is here in our bathtub.
He has a bubble beard.

Aretha tilted her head. Her ears were on alert. When she sniffed the air, her wet nose quivered.

"Begone, foul beast," said Crenshaw.

Aretha plopped her big paws on the edge of the tub and gave Crenshaw a heartfelt, slobbery kiss.

He hissed, long and slow. It sounded more like a bike tire losing air than an angry cat.

Aretha tried for another kiss. Crenshaw flicked a pawful of bubbles at her. She caught them in her mouth and ate them.

"I never have seen the point of dogs," said Crenshaw.

"You're not real," I said again.

"You always were a stubborn child."

Crenshaw unplugged the tub and stood. Bubbles drifted. Bathwater swirled. Dripping wet, he looked half his size. With his fur slicked down, I could make out the delicate bones of his legs. Water rushed past them like a flood around trees.

He had excellent posture.

I didn't remember Crenshaw towering above me. I'd gotten a lot taller since I was seven, but had he? Did imaginary friends actually grow?

"Towel, please," said Crenshaw.

14

With trembling fingers, I passed Robin's faded pink Hello Kitty towel to Crenshaw.

Thoughts zapped through my brain like summer lightning.

I can see my imaginary friend.

I can hear him.

I can talk to him.

He is using a towel.

As Crenshaw climbed out of the tub, he reached

for my hand. His paw was warm and soft and wet, big as a lion's, with fingers the size of baby carrots.

I can feel him.

He feels real.

He smells like wet cat.

He has fingers.

Cats do not have fingers.

Crenshaw attempted to dry himself. Each time he noticed a tuft of hair out of place, he paused to lick it. His tongue was covered with little prickers, like pink Velcro.

"Those things on your tongue are called papillae," I said, and then I realized that maybe this wasn't the best time to be sharing nature facts.

Crenshaw glanced in the mirror. "My, don't I look a fright."

Aretha licked his tail helpfully.

"Off me, hound," Crenshaw said. He tossed the towel aside, and it landed on Aretha. "I need more than a towel. I need a good old-fashioned shake."

Crenshaw took a deep breath. His body rippled.

Water droplets flew like crystal fireworks. When he'd finished, his fur was spiky.

Aretha tossed off the towel, wagging crazily.

"Look at that ridiculous tail," Crenshaw said. "Humans laugh with their mouths, dogs with their tails. Either way, it makes for pointless mirth."

I pulled the towel away from Aretha. She snared it between her teeth to play tug-of-war. "What about cats?" I asked. "Don't you laugh?"

I am talking to a cat.

A cat is talking to me.

"We smirk," Crenshaw said. "We sneer. Rarely, we are quietly amused." He licked his paw and smoothed a spike of fur near his ear. "But we do not laugh."

"I need to sit down," I said.

"Where are your parents? And Robin? I haven't seen them in ages."

"Sleeping."

"I shall go wake them."

"No!" I practically screamed it. "I mean . . . let's go to my room. We need to talk."

"I'll leap onto their beds and walk on their heads. It will be amusing."

"No," I said. "You will not walk on anyone's head."

Crenshaw reached for the doorknob. His paw slipped off when he tried to turn it. "Would you mind?" he said.

I grabbed the knob. "Listen," I said. "I need to know something. Can everybody see you? Or just me?"

Crenshaw chewed on one of his nails. It was pale and pink, sharp as a new moon sliver. "I can't say for sure, Jackson. I'm a bit out of practice."

"Out of practice doing what?"

"Being your friend." He moved to another nail. "Theoretically, only you can see me. But when an imaginary friend is left to his own devices, alone and forgotten . . . who knows?" His voice trailed off. He made a pouty face, far better than anything Robin could pull off. "It's been a long time since you left me behind. Perhaps things have changed. Perhaps the fabric of the universe has unraveled just a tad."

"Well, what if you *are* visible? I can't let you just walk down the hall to my room. What if my dad wakes up to get a snack? What if Robin has to go to the bathroom?"

"She doesn't have a litter box in her room?"

"No. She does not have a litter box in her room." I pointed to the toilet.

"Ah, yes. It's all coming back to me now."

"Look, we're going to my room. Be quiet. And if anybody comes out, just, I don't know, freeze. Pretend you're a stuffed animal."

"Stuffed?" He sounded offended. "I beg your pardon?"

"Just do what I say."

The hallway was dark, except for the bathroom light spilling onto the carpet like melted butter. Crenshaw moved silently, for such a big guy. That's why cats are amazing hunters.

I heard a soft creak behind me.

Robin stepped out of her bedroom.

I jerked my head to check on Crenshaw.

He froze in place. His mouth was open and his teeth were bared, like one of those dusty, dead animals on display at a natural-history museum.

"Jacks?" said Robin in a slurry voice. "Who were you talking to?"

15

"Uh . . . Aretha," I said. "I was talking to Aretha."

I hated lying. But it wasn't like I had a choice.

Robin yawned. "Were you giving her a bath?"

"Yeah."

I looked back and forth, forth and back.

Sister.

Imaginary friend.

Sister.

Imaginary friend.

Aretha ran over to nuzzle Robin's hand.

"Aretha's not wet," Robin said.

"I used the hair dryer on her."

"She hates the hair dryer." Robin kissed the top of Aretha's head. "Don't you, baby?"

Robin didn't seem to see Crenshaw. Maybe because it was pretty dark in the hallway. Or maybe because he was invisible.

Or maybe because none of this was really happening.

"She smells the same," Robin observed. "Nice and doggy."

I glanced at Crenshaw. He rolled his eyes.

"Oh well," Robin said, yawning. "I'm going back to bed. Night, Jacks. Love you."

"Night, Robin," I said. "Love you, too."

As soon as her bedroom door closed, we retreated to my room. Crenshaw leaped onto my mattress as if he owned it. When Aretha tried to join him, he growled. It wasn't very convincing.

"I need to understand what's happening." I slumped against the wall. "Am I going crazy?"

Crenshaw's tail rose and fell, making lazy Ss in the air. "No, you most certainly are not." He licked a paw. "By the way, at the risk of repeating myself, how about those purple jelly beans?"

When I didn't answer, he settled into a doughnut shape, tail wrapped around himself, and closed his eyes. He purred the way my dad snores, like a motorboat with engine problems.

I stared at him, a huge, damp, bubble bath–taking cat.

There's always a logical explanation, I told myself. And a part of me, the scientist part of me, really wanted to figure out what was going on.

Still, a much bigger part of me felt certain that I needed this hallucination—this dream—this *thing*—to disappear. Later, when Crenshaw was safely out of my house, not to mention my brain, I could think about what all this meant.

A soft knock on my door told me Robin was back. She always knocks the beginning of "Wheels on the Bus": *Tap-tap-ta-ta-tap.*

"Jackson?"

"*Please* go to sleep, Robin."

"I can't sleep. I miss my trash can."

"Your trash can?"

"Dad took my trash can to sell at the yard sale."

"I'm pretty sure that was a mistake, Robin," I said. "Nobody wants to buy your trash can."

"It had blue bunnies on it."

"We'll get it out of the garage in the morning."

Aretha made a move to sniff Crenshaw's tail. He hissed.

I put my finger to my lips to shush him, but Robin didn't seem to hear anything.

"Night, Robin," I said. "See you in the morning."

"Jackson?"

I rubbed my eyes and groaned, the way I'd seen my parents do more than once. "*Now* what?"

"Do you think I can get another bed someday?"

"Sure. Of course. Maybe even one with blue bunnies."

"Jackson?"

"Yes?"

"My room is scary without my stuff in it. Could you come read me Lyle?"

I took a long, slow breath. "Sure. I'll be right there."

Robin sniffled. "I'll just wait right here by your door. 'Kay?"

"Okay." I shot a glance at Crenshaw. "Just give me a second, Robin. There's something I really need to do."

16

I went to my window and opened it. Carefully, I pulled out the screen. Our apartment was on the ground floor. A few feet below the window, a cushion of grass waited.

"Good-bye, Crenshaw," I said.

He opened one eye a bit, like someone peeking from behind a shade. "But we were having such a lovely time."

"Now," I said. I put my hands on my hips to show I meant business.

"Jackson, be reasonable. I came all this way."

"You have to go back to wherever you came from."

Crenshaw opened his other eye. "But you need me here."

"I don't need you. I have enough to deal with already."

With a great show of effort, Crenshaw sat up. He stretched, easing his back into an upside-down U. "I don't think you understand what's going on here, Jackson," he said. "Imaginary friends don't come of their own volition. We are invited. We stay as long as we're needed. And then, and only then, do we leave."

"Well, I sure didn't invite you."

Crenshaw sent me a doubtful look. His long, whiskery brows moved like strings on a marionette.

I took a step closer. "If you won't go, I'll make you go."

I put my arms around his waist and yanked. It was like hugging a lion. That cat weighed a ton.

Crenshaw dug his claws deep into the quilt my great-aunt Trudy made when I was a baby. I gave up and let go.

"Look," Crenshaw said as he extracted his claws from my quilt, "I can't go until I help you. I don't make the rules."

"Then who does?"

Crenshaw stared at me with eyes like green marbles. He put his two front paws on my shoulders. He smelled like soapsuds and catnip and the ocean at night.

"You do, Jackson," he said. "*You* make the rules."

A foghorn bleated in the distance. I pointed to the windowsill. "I don't need anyone's help. And I sure don't need an imaginary friend. I'm not a little kid anymore."

"Balderdash. Is this because I hissed at that odorous dog?"

"No."

"Could we at least wait till morning? There's a chill in the air, and I just took a bubble bath."

"No."

Tap-tap-ta-ta-tap. "Jacks? It's lonely in this hallway."

"Coming, Robin," I called.

Out of the corner of my eye, I noticed a frog hop onto the windowsill. He gave a tiny, nervous croak.

"We have a visitor," I said, pointing. Maybe if I distracted Crenshaw he'd move on. "Did you know some frogs can leap so far it'd be like a human jumping the length of a football field? They're amazing jumpers."

"Mmm. They're amazing bedtime snacks, too," murmured Crenshaw. "Come to think of it, I wouldn't mind a little amphibious morsel."

I could see he was in full predator mode. His eyes turned to dark pools. His rear wiggled. His tail twitched.

"See you, Crenshaw," I said.

"Fine, Jackson," he whispered, eyes lasering in on the frog. "You win. I'll leave, do bit of hunting. I am, after all, a creature of the night. Meantime, you get to work."

I crossed my arms over my chest. "On what, exactly?"

"The facts. You need to tell the truth, my friend." The frog twitched, and Crenshaw froze, pure muscle and instinct.

"Which facts? Tell the truth to who?"

Crenshaw pulled his gaze off the frog. He looked at me, and to my surprise, I saw tenderness in his eyes. "To the person who matters most of all."

The frog jumped off the sill, back into the night. In one magnificent leap, Crenshaw followed. When I ran to the window, all I saw was a blur of black and white, streaking through the moon-tipped grass.

I felt like I'd taken off an itchy sweater on a cold day: relieved to be rid of it, but surprised by how chilly the air turned out to be.

17

Robin was waiting for me in the hallway, sitting crisscross-applesauce. Her stuffed armadillo, Spot, was in her lap.

I took her hand and led her back to her bedroom. Her rainbow nightlight painted stripes on the ceiling. I wished I had one in my room, although I'd never admit it.

"I heard you talking," she said as she crawled under her blanket.

"Sometimes I talk to myself."

"That's kind of weird." Robin yawned.

"Yeah," I said, tucking her in. "It is."

"You promised Lyle," she reminded me.

I'd been hoping she'd forgotten. "Yep."

"He's in my keepsakes bag."

I rummaged around in the brown paper bag. A bald doll poked out of the top, sizing me up with blank and beady eyes.

"Scooch over," I said. Robin made room for me on her mattress.

I opened the book. Its pages were soft, its cover tattered.

"Robin," I asked, "have you ever had an imaginary friend?"

"You mean like inbisible?"

"Invisible. Yeah. Like that."

"Nope."

"Really? Never?"

"Nope. I have LaSandra and Jimmy and Kylie.

And sometimes Josh when he's not being a booger-head. They're real, so I don't need to pretend."

I flipped through the pages of the book. "But sometimes, you know, when you're alone?" I paused. I wasn't sure exactly what I wanted to ask. "Like say you're home and you don't have any friends over and you really need to talk to someone who'll listen. Not even then?"

"Nope." She smiled. "'Cause anyways I have you."

It made me happy to hear her say that. But somehow it wasn't quite the answer I'd been hoping for.

I opened to the first page. "'This is the house. The house on East 88th Street. It is empty now—'"

"Like our house," Robin interrupted. "Only we live in a 'partment."

"True."

"Jacks?" Robin said softly. "Remember when we lived in the minivan for a while?"

"Do you really remember that? You were just little."

"Kinda I remember but not really." Robin made Spot do a little dance on her blanket. "But you told me about it. So I was wondering."

"Wondering what?"

Spot performed a backflip. "Wondering if we're going to have to live there again. Because where would we go to the bathroom?"

I couldn't believe it. Robin was just a kid. How had she figured out so much? Did she spy on our parents the way I did?

Robin sniffled. She wiped her eyes with Spot. I realized she was crying without making any noise.

"I . . . I miss my things and I don't want to live in a car with no potty and also my tummy keeps growling," she whispered.

I knew what to tell her. She needed to hear the facts. We were having money problems. We were probably going to have to leave our apartment. We might even end up back in our minivan. There was a good chance she'd have to leave all her friends behind.

I put my arm around Robin and hugged her close. She looked up at me. Her eyes shimmered.

You need to tell the truth, my friend.

"Don't be ridiculous," I said. "We can't live in our car. Where would we put Popsicles? Besides, Aretha and Dad snore like crazy."

She laughed, just a little.

"You worry too much, girl. Everything's fine. I promise. Now let's get back to Lyle."

Another sniffle. A nod.

"Hey, fun fact about crocodiles," I said. "Did you know that a bunch of them in the water is called a 'float'?"

Robin didn't answer. She was already sound asleep, snoring softly.

Me, I couldn't sleep. I was too busy remembering.

PART TWO

Mashed potatoes are to give everybody enough

—A HOLE IS TO DIG:

A FIRST BOOK OF FIRST DEFINITIONS,

written by Ruth Krauss and

illustrated by Maurice Sendak

PART TWO

18

I guess becoming homeless doesn't happen all at once.

My mom told me once that money problems sort of sneak up on you. She said it's like catching a cold. At first you just have a tickle in your throat, and then you have a headache, and then maybe you're coughing a little. The next thing you know, you have a pile of Kleenexes around your bed and you're hacking your lungs up.

Maybe we didn't become homeless overnight. But

that's what it felt like. I was finishing first grade. My dad had been sick. My mom had lost her teaching job. And all of sudden—*bam*—we weren't living in a nice house with a swing set in the backyard anymore.

At least that's how I remember it. But like I said before, memory is weird. It seems like I should have thought to myself, Whoa, I'm going to miss my house and my neighborhood and my friends and my life.

But all I remember thinking was how much fun living in our minivan was going to be.

19

We moved out of our house right after first grade ended. There was no big announcement, no good-bye party. We just sort of left, the way you abandon your desk at the end of the school year. You clean it out, but if you leave a few pencils and an old spelling test behind, you don't worry about it too much. You know the kid who has your desk next fall will take care of things.

My parents didn't own a lot of stuff, but they still

managed to fill our minivan. You could hardly see out the windows. I saved my pillow and backpack to load last. I was putting them onto the rear seat when I noticed something odd.

Someone had left the back windshield wiper on, even though it was a sunny day. No rain, no clouds, no nothing.

Back. Forth. Back. Forth.

My parents were packing odds and ends in the house, and Robin was with them. I was all alone.

Back. Forth. Back. Forth.

I looked closer. The wiper was long and awfully hairy.

It looked a lot more like a tail than a windshield wiper.

I leaped out and ran to the rear. I saw the dent in the fender from the time my dad backed into a shopping cart at Costco. I saw the bumper sticker my mom had used to cover the dent. It said I BRAKE FOR DINOSAURS.

I saw the windshield wiper.

But it wasn't moving. And it wasn't hairy.

And right then I knew, the way you know that it's going to rain long before the first drop splatters on your nose, that something was about to change.

20

When the minivan was packed, we stood in the parking lot. Nobody wanted to get in.

"Why don't I drive, Tom?" said my mom. "You were in a lot of pain this morning—"

"I'm fine," my dad said firmly. "Fit as a fiddle. Whatever that means."

My mom strapped Robin into her car seat, and we climbed into the minivan. The seats were hot from the sun.

"This is only for a few days," said my mom, adjusting her sunglasses.

"Two weeks tops," said my dad. "Maybe three. Or four."

"We just need to catch up a little." My mom was using her there's-nothing-wrong voice, so I knew something was really wrong. "Pretty soon we'll find a new apartment."

"I liked our house," I said.

"Apartments are nice, too," said my mom.

"I don't get why we can't just stay."

"It's complicated," said my dad.

"You'll understand when you're older, Jackson," said my mom.

"Play Wiggles," Robin yelled, squirming in her car seat. She loved the Wiggles, a group that wrote silly songs for kids.

"First a little hitting-the-road music, Robin," said my dad. "Then Wiggles." He slipped a CD into the car player. It was one of my mom and dad's favorite singers. His name was B.B. King.

My mom and dad like a kind of music called "blues." In a blues song, somebody's sad about something. Like maybe they broke up with their girlfriend or they lost all their money or they missed a train to a faraway place. But the weird thing is, when you hear the songs, you feel happy.

My dad makes up lots of crazy blues songs. Robin's favorite was "Ain't No PB in My PB&J." Mine was called "Downside-Up Vampire Bat Boogie," about a bat who couldn't sleep upside down, like bats are supposed to do.

I'd never heard the B.B. King song my dad had chosen to play. It was about how nobody loved this guy except his mother.

"What's he mean about how even his mom could be jiving him, Dad?" I asked.

"Jiving means lying. It's funny, see, because your mom and dad *always* love you."

"Except when you don't floss," said my mom.

I was quiet for a while. "Do kids always have to love their mom and dad?" I asked.

97

I caught my dad's reflection in the rearview mirror. He looked back at me with a question in his eyes.

"Put it this way," he said. "You can be mad at someone and still love them with all your heart."

We pulled out of the driveway. Aretha sat between Robin and me. She was only a few months old, and still had her puppy-soft fur and clumsy paws.

Our neighbor Mr. Sera was cutting yellow roses from his garden. We'd already said official goodbyes. He waved and we waved back, like we were on our way to the Grand Canyon or Disney World.

"Does Mr. Sera have a cat?" I asked. "A really big cat?"

"Just Mabel," my mom answered. "The Chihuahua with an attitude. Why?"

I glanced back at the rear windshield, but it was blocked by boxes and bags.

"No reason," I said.

My dad cranked up the volume on B.B. King, who was still pretty sure nobody loved him, including his mom.

Aretha cocked her head and howled. She liked to sing along, especially to blues songs. Although she liked the Wiggles too.

We drove a few blocks. My lower lip quivered, but I didn't cry.

My mom sighed softly. "Let the adventure begin," she said.

21

If you ever have to live in your car, you are going to have some problems with feet. Especially if you're stuck in there with your little sister and your mom and your dad and your puppy and your imaginary friend.

There are many kinds of feet problems.

Stinky dad feet.

The Magic Marker smell of nail polish on your

mom's toes because she says she still wants to look nice so please just deal with it.

Sister feet kicking you just as you're falling asleep.

The scratchy surprise of dog feet trying to wake you up.

Imaginary friend feet tiptoeing on your head.

I thought hard about the feet problem. Finally I came up with a plan. What's the worst that can happen, is how I figured it.

What I did is I took a cardboard TV box we found behind Wal-Mart. I smushed it flat. I drew on the outside of the box and the inside too. I only had three markers and one dried out when the cap fell under the backseat. So it was mostly just red dogs with blue eyes. And blue cats with red eyes.

I put stars on the inside. They seemed like a good thing to think about before you went to sleep.

I wrote kep out jacksons rum on the top. Mom said, too bad we had to leave our dictionary behind. Dad said, if only it really was rum.

Every night I opened up my box and slipped my

sleeping bag inside it. When I crawled inside, I felt like a caterpillar in a cocoon. It was almost like my old room, where I could think without anyone bugging me.

When Robin kicked me in her sleep, she hit the box. Which was not exactly the same as kicking me.

Unfortunately, Aretha liked to sleep with me. So it could get a little dog-breath-y.

Also, the box didn't help much with the stinky dad feet.

I knew we were lucky because we had our old Honda minivan, which had lots of room. I met a kid who lived for a whole year in one of those VW cars. It was red and round like a ladybug and just about as tiny. The poor kid had to sleep sitting up, squished between his two little sisters.

Another reason we were lucky was because my sleeping box was just decoration. Some people actually live in boxes on the street.

I wasn't looking on the bright side. It's better to have a big car than a little one when you are living in it. And it's better to have a box in a car than a box on a street.

Those were just facts.

I wasn't like my dad, who kept saying we weren't homeless.

We were just car camping.

22

I didn't think much about the cat tail–windshield wiper for a while. Things were so weird I guess I didn't want to add any extra weirdness.

Our first night in the minivan was kind of fun. We drove to a park near the Golden Gate Bridge. A man had a telescope to look at the sky, and he showed us the Big Dipper and Orion. Across the water, the lights of San Francisco covered the ground like lazy stars.

We were going to just sleep in the parking lot. But a security guy knocked on the window. He told us we had to get moving, and then he waved his flashlight around like a Star Wars lightsaber.

We drove to Denny's, a restaurant that's open 24 hours. My mom knew one of the cooks, and he asked the manager if we could park there for just one night. He said yes and even let us have some pancakes that were too burnt for the customers.

We had more burnt pancakes in the morning. By then everybody was grumpy and sore. Only Aretha was in a good mood. She loves pancakes.

My parents didn't have any work scheduled that day, so we headed to the public library to kill time and wash up. My mom and dad took turns staying outside with Aretha. It's dangerous to leave a dog in a hot car.

The library had air-conditioning and soft chairs. The bathrooms were clean, which was a nice plus.

I never used to think about things like is a bathroom clean or not. Whenever I took a bath, my mom would say, "Here comes Hurricane Jackson," because I made such a mess.

One of my favorite bath experiments is about something scientists call buoyancy. Will It Float? is what I call it. It can get a little messy but it's very interesting. For example, if you drop a mostly full bottle of ketchup in the tub, it will not float. But it will turn the water an awesome color.

It will also annoy your mom.

We stayed at the library most of the day. The librarian in the children's department even shared her sandwich with Robin and me. She had Ritz crackers, too, and she gave all of those to Robin.

After that, Robin decided she was going to be a librarian when she grew up. If the animal scientist thing doesn't work out, I might become a librarian too.

23

We'd only been living in our van for four days when somebody stole my mom's purse, which had most of our money in it because my dad's wallet was falling apart.

After we told a policeman, he wanted to know our address so if they found the money they could give it back.

We are between addresses is what my mom told him.

"Ah," said the policeman. He nodded like he'd figured out a hard math problem.

My parents and the policeman talked for a while. He gave them the address of two homeless shelters where people can sleep at night. The dads go to one place and the moms and kids go to another, he explained.

"No way," said my dad. "Not happening."

Robin said, "We are car camping."

The policeman looked at Aretha, who was licking his shiny black shoe.

He said that no animals were allowed at either shelter.

I asked if that included puppies.

"Sadly," he said.

I told him my teacher Mr. Vandermeer had pet rats.

"Rats are especially not allowed," said the policeman.

There are good rats and bad rats, I told him. I said white rats like the ones my teacher had, Harry and Hermione, were very clean animals. But wild rats could make you sick.

Then I told the policeman how Mr. Vandermeer was teaching his rats to play basketball with a teeny ball for a science experiment. Rats are amazingly intelligent.

"Basketball," the policeman repeated. He looked at my parents like maybe they should be worried about me. Then he gave my mom a little white card with phone numbers on it.

"Social services, shelters, food pantry, free clinic," he said. "Check back with us about the theft. Meantime, hang in there, folks."

We were almost to the car when I heard the policeman call, "Hey, Ratman!"

I turned around. He waved me back. When I got there he said, "How's their jump shot? The rats, I mean?"

"Not so good," I said. "But they're kind of learning. They get treats when they do something right. It's called 'posi—'" I couldn't remember. It was two long words.

"Positive reinforcement?"

"Yep!"

"Yeah, I could use some of that myself," said the policeman.

He reached into his pocket and pulled out a crumpled twenty-dollar bill. "Give this to your dad," he said. "But wait until you're in the car."

I asked how come I had to wait.

"Because otherwise he'll give it right back to me," the policeman said.

"How do you know?" I asked.

"I know," he said.

When I was inside the car, I gave the money to my dad. He looked like he was going to throw it out the window.

I thought maybe he was going to yell at me, but he didn't. He just tapped his fingers on the steering wheel. *Tap. Tap. Tap.*

Finally he shoved the bill in his jeans pocket.

"Looks like dinner's on me," he said softly.

24

The next day, we dropped my mom at her part-time waitress job. Before she got out of the car, she looked at my dad and said, "We have to apply for assistance, Tom."

"We'll be back on our feet before they deal with all the paperwork," he said.

"Still."

"Plus we probably make too much money to qualify for help."

"Still."

They looked at each other for a few long seconds. Finally my dad nodded.

We went to an office called Social Services to find out about help. My dad filled out lots of forms while Robin and I sat on hard orange chairs. Then we went to three hardware stores, where my dad put in applications for work. My dad grumbled about all the gas we used up. To cheer him up, I said maybe we could feed the car water instead. He laughed a little then.

"Not having enough work is tough work," my dad told my mom when she joined us in the car after her shift. He took a deep breath and blew it out hard, like he was facing a birthday cake with too many candles.

"Dad?" I said. "I'm kind of hungry."

"Me too, buddy," he said. "Me too."

"Almost forgot," my mom said, reaching into her tote bag. "I grabbed some of the bagels that the chef was about to throw out." She pulled out a white paper sack. "They're pretty stale, though. And they're pumpernickel."

"Well, that's a start," said my dad. He stared out the window. After a moment, he clapped his hands. "Okay. Let's get this show on the road. Guess I can't stall any longer."

My mom touched his shoulder. "Are you sure about this, Tom?" she asked. "I get my paycheck tomorrow. We could go to the food pantry. Or the shelter."

"Nope. I got this." He smiled, but it didn't look like a real smile to me. "I'd rather do a little performing than stand in another endless line at some office, waiting for a handout."

We drove to the back of the restaurant. My dad found a nice clean box in the Dumpster.

"Are you making the begging sign?" I asked him. He'd been talking about it off and on with my mom since our money was stolen.

"Given that I'll be singing for our supper," he said

as he tore the box into pieces, "I prefer to call it a request for gratuities."

"What's a gratuity?" I asked.

"A tip. Money you give someone like a waiter," my mom said. "When we were young, your dad and I used to be street performers, before we had regular gigs. Lots of musicians do it."

"I've got this down to a science," said my dad. "First off, you need a cardboard sign. Then you need a busy intersection. The best corners have long stoplights."

"It might not hurt to take Aretha," my mom said.

"People love dogs," I told my dad. "I bet you'll make a lot more money with a dog."

"Can I borrow a marker, Jackson?" my dad asked.

I handed him my blue marker. "That guy on the corner by Target? He has a puppy."

My dad studied a cardboard rectangle. "No prop puppies."

"Write 'God Bless,' at least," said my mom. "Everybody writes 'God Bless.'"

"Nope. As it happens, I have no idea what God is up to."

My mom sighed.

My dad scribbled something on the cardboard, like he was in a hurry to be somewhere else. He held up the sign and asked what we thought.

I didn't answer right away. In second grade, my dad got a D in penmanship, which is how you make your letters. He did not improve with age.

"What's it say?" I asked.

" 'THANK YOU.' "

"Looks a lot like 'THINK YOU.' "

He shrugged. "Even better."

25

We drove to a busy corner and parked next to a Starbucks. It was a cool-and-rainy kind of day.

"Are you sure about this?" my mom asked. "Let me join you."

"Won't be the first time I've played an outdoor concert," my dad said. "And you can't come with me. Someone needs to stay with the kids."

We waited in the minivan, watching him as he

crossed the street. He had his sign and his guitar, but no Aretha.

My dad stood on the lane divider by the left-hand turn signal. He propped his THANK YOU sign against his open guitar case. We couldn't hear him singing. There was too much traffic.

"He needs to make eye contact," my mom said.

The light turned red and a line of cars formed next to my dad. Someone beeped his horn, and my dad looked over. A driver in a taxi passed him some money.

The next time the light was red, a driver in a pickup truck gave my dad coins. When the light turned green, people mostly just passed by, their eyes on the road ahead. But a few smiled or nodded.

Red. Green. Red. Green. The hour wore on. When he climbed back into our van, my dad smelled like car exhaust. He passed my mom a handful of wadded-up bills and some coins. "Seven lousy bucks and change."

"It's really starting to come down," my mom said.

"People don't like to open their windows when it rains." She gazed at the wet dollars. "We could try up by the mall. Maybe it's just a bad corner."

My dad shook his head. "Maybe it's a bad idea."

"We need the rain," I said. "Because of the drought and all."

"Good point," said my dad. "Let's look on Jackson's bright side."

After a while, the rain slowed to a drizzle. We drove to a park so my mom and Robin could get some fresh air. She said Robin was going stir-crazy.

"How about you come, too, Jackson?" my mom asked as she undid Robin's car seat straps.

"Nah. Too wet," I said.

"You're both gonna get wet," my dad warned.

"Robin's getting antsy," my mom said. "We can dry our clothes on top of the car when the sun comes out."

"Day just gets better and better."

My mom leaned across the seat and kissed my dad's cheek, which was kind of stubbly. "Good times," she said.

I stayed in our minivan with my dad. Aretha, who smelled a little ripe, was sleeping in the back.

I decided to draw a new sign for my dad. A better one, like the one my mom had made for our bathroom door.

I tore some cardboard off the end of my sleeping box. Then I made a smiling fish, sitting in a canoe. He was holding a fishing pole and wearing a floppy hat.

In big letters I wrote: ID RATHIR BE FISHING.

My dad was dozing in the driver's seat. His eyes were closed, but he wasn't snoring. So I knew he wasn't serious.

I poked him with my sign.

"Try this next time, Dad."

He blinked, rubbed his eyes, and took the sign from me. For a long time, he just stared at it.

"Great job," he finally said. "I like the mustache on the trout. Nice touch. Just FYI, *RATHER* has an *E*. And *ID* . . . oh, never mind. It's great, kiddo. Thanks."

"If it gets wet, we can grab some more cardboard, and I'll make a new one."

My dad set the sign down gently on the passenger seat. Then he opened the door and stepped outside. It was misty. Leaves were shiny and dripping.

Mom says she's only seen my dad cry three times. When they got married, and when Robin and I were born.

I watched my dad lean against the hood of our car and cover his eyes with his hand.

His face was damp, but I told myself it was probably just the rain.

26

During the afternoon rush hour the next day, my dad returned to the same corner with his new sign. It was drizzling again, and gray clouds hung low in the sky. I waited in the car with my mom and Robin and Aretha.

My mom had just gotten off work at Rite Aid. She said two people were out sick, which meant she was the only cashier. People in line were grumpy, she said. Why didn't they just read the *Enquirer* and wait their turns?

A driver in a red SUV rolled down his window. He smiled and said something to my dad. They both nodded. My dad tucked the sign under his arm and held out his hands till they were about two feet apart.

"I'll bet Dad's telling him about that trout at the lake," I said to my mom.

She smiled. "And exaggerating."

"Is that the same as lying?" I asked.

"Not when it's fish-related," said my mom.

When the light changed, the driver handed my dad money and waved as he pulled away. After about an hour, he'd collected a bunch of dollar bills. Also a big cup of coffee and a sack with two slices of lemon pound cake in it.

My sign was a soggy mess.

My mom flattened the bills on her lap. "Fifty-six dollars," she announced.

"And eighty-three cents," my dad added.

My parents shared the coffee. I split the pound

cake with Robin. Then I climbed to the back. Aretha was tail-thumping hopefully.

When no one was looking, I gave her my whole piece.

It was windy and cold, and the rain had come back hard. We listened to the radio as tiny rivers zigged and zagged down the glass.

A new man went to stand on the corner. His sign said VET—GOD BLESS. A small, poodley-looking dog was nestled in his half-zipped jacket.

"I still think you should take Aretha with you next time, Dad," I said. "I'll bet we'll make even more money."

He didn't answer. I figured he was listening to the radio announcer. She was warning that the chance of rain was 80 percent, so it was a good night to stay inside.

A summer-day-camp bus stopped at the light. Its windows were fogged up. I saw some kids and hunched down in case I knew them.

Someone had drawn a smiley face with a word by

it. *Hello!* I decided, but it was hard to tell. I was on the outside, so everything was backward.

Aretha licked my sticky hand.

"Next time," my mom said, leaning her head on my dad's shoulder, "I'll do it."

"No," he answered, so softly I almost couldn't hear him. "No, you won't."

27

The next evening, Crenshaw appeared. All of him. Not just his tail.

We were at a rest stop off Highway 101, sitting at a picnic table.

"Cheetos and water for dinner," my mom said. She sighed. "I am a bad, bad mother."

"Not a lot of options at a vending machine on the 101," my dad said. He had hung a pair of his underwear on a nearby bush to dry. Sometimes we washed our clothes in the sinks at bathrooms. I tried not to look at the underwear.

After we ate, I headed to a patch of grass under a pine tree. I lay down and stared at the darkening sky. I could see my parents, and they could see me, but at least I felt like I was a little bit on my own.

I loved my family. But I was also tired of my family. I was tired of being hungry. I was tired of sleeping in a box.

I missed my bed. I missed my books and Legos. I even missed my bathtub.

Those were the facts.

A gentle breeze set the grass dancing. The stars spun.

I heard the sound of wheels on gravel and sat up on my elbows. I recognized the tail first.

"Meow," said the cat.

"Meow," I said back, because it seemed polite.

28

We lived in our minivan for fourteen weeks.

Some days we drove from place to place. Some days we just parked and sat. We weren't going anywhere. We just knew we weren't going home.

I guess getting *out* of homelessness doesn't happen all at once, either.

We were lucky. Some people live in their cars for years.

I'm not looking on the bright side. It was pretty scary. And stinky.

But my parents took care of us the best they could.

After a month, my dad got a part-time job at a hardware store. My mom picked up some extra wait-ressing shifts, and my dad kept singing for tips. Every time his fishing sign got wet, I made him a new one. Slowly they started saving money, bit by bit, to pay for a rental deposit on an apartment.

It was sort of like getting over a cold. Sometimes you feel like you'll never stop coughing. Other times you're sure tomorrow is the day you'll definitely be well.

When they finally put together enough money, my parents moved us to Swanlake Village. It was about forty miles from our old house, which meant I had to start at a new school. I didn't care at all. At least I was going back to school. A place where facts mattered and things made sense.

Instead of a house, we moved into a small,

tired-looking apartment. It seemed like a palace to us. A place where you could be warm and dry and safe.

I started school late, but eventually I made new friends. I never told them about the time we were homeless. Not even Marisol. I just couldn't.

If I never talked about it, I felt like it couldn't ever happen again.

29

Crenshaw and I didn't chat much during those weeks on the road. There was always someone around to interrupt us. But that was okay. I knew he was there and that was enough.

Sometimes that's all you really need from a friend.

When I think about that time, what I remember most of all is Crenshaw, riding on top of our mini-van. I'd stare out the window at the world blurring past, and every so often I'd catch a glimpse of his tail, riding the wind like the end of a kite.

I'd feel hopeful then, for a while at least, that things would get better, that maybe, just maybe, anything was possible.

30

I guess for most kids, imaginary friends just sort of fade away, the way dreams do. I've asked people when their imaginary friends stopped hanging around, and they never seem to remember.

Everybody said the same thing: I guess I just outgrew him.

But I lost Crenshaw all of a sudden, after things got back to normal. It was like when you have a favorite T-shirt that you've worn forever. One day you put it on, and surprise: Your belly button is showing. You don't remember growing too big for your shirt, but sure enough, there's your belly button, sticking out for the whole wide world to see.

The day he left, Crenshaw walked to school with me. He did that most mornings unless he wanted to stay home and watch *Blue's Clues* reruns. We stopped at the playground. I was telling him about how I wanted to get a real cat someday.

That was before I found out my parents are extremely allergic to cats.

Crenshaw stood on his head. Then he did a cartwheel. He was an excellent cartwheeler.

When he came to a stop, he gave me a grumpy look. "*I'm* a cat," he said.

"I know," I said.

"I'm a *real* cat." His tail whipped up and down.

"I mean," I said, "you know—a cat other people can see."

He batted a paw at a yellow butterfly. I could tell he was ignoring me.

A bunch of big guys, fourth and fifth graders, walked by. They pointed at me and laughed, making cuckoo circles with their fingers.

"Who you talking to, doofus?" one asked, and then he snort-laughed.

That is my least favorite kind of laughing.

I pretended not to hear him. I knelt down and tied my shoe like it was a very important thing I had to do.

My face was hot. My eyes were wet. I'd never been embarrassed about having an imaginary friend until that moment.

I waited. The boys moved on. Then I heard someone else approaching. She wasn't walking. More like skip-dancing.

"Hey, I'm Marisol," said the girl. I'd seen her at recess before. She had long, dark, crazy hair and an unusually large smile. "I have a Tyrannosaurus backpack just like yours. I'm going to be a paleontologist when I grow up, which means—"

"I know what it means," I said. "I want to be one too. Or maybe a bat scientist."

Her smile got even bigger.

"I'm Jackson," I said, and I stood.

When I looked around me, I realized that Crenshaw had vanished.

31

I've sometimes wondered if I was kind of old to have an imaginary friend. Crenshaw didn't even show up in my life until the end of first grade.

So one day at the library, I looked it up. Turns out somebody did a study on children and their imaginary friends. Fact is, 31 percent of them had an imaginary friend at age six or seven, even more than three- and four-year-olds.

Maybe I wasn't so old after all.

In any case, Crenshaw had excellent timing. He came into my life just when I needed him to.

It was a good time to have a friend, even if he was imaginary.

PART THREE

The world is so you have something to stand on

—A HOLE IS TO DIG:

A FIRST BOOK OF FIRST DEFINITIONS,

written by Ruth Krauss and

illustrated by Maurice Sendak

32

It occurred to me that Crenshaw's return—the night of the kitty bubble bath, as I came to think of it— might be a sign that I was right about my parents. It was coming again—the moving, the craziness. Maybe even the homelessness.

I told myself I'd just have to face facts and make the best of it. It wouldn't be the first time we'd hit a rough spot.

Still and all. I'd been hoping to get Ms. Leach for fifth grade. Everybody said she liked to explode stuff for science experiments. And Marisol and I had our dog-walking business going pretty well. And I'd been looking forward to trying out the new skate park when they got it built in January. And maybe even doing rec soccer, if we could come up with the money for a uniform.

It would be easier for Robin. You could move her anywhere and she'd be fine. She made friends in an instant. She didn't have to worry about real stuff.

She was still a kid.

I lay on my mattress as the list of things I was going to miss kept getting longer. I told my brain to take a time-out. Sometimes that actually works.

Not so much, this round.

Last year, my principal told me I was an "old soul." I asked what that meant, and he said I seemed wise beyond my years. He said it was a compliment. That he liked the way I always knew when someone needed help with fractions. Or the way I emptied the pencil sharpener without being asked.

That's the way I am at home, too. Most of the

time, anyway. Sometimes I feel like the most grown-up one in the house. Which is why it seemed like my parents should have known they could talk to me about grown-up stuff.

And why it seemed like they should tell me the truth about moving.

Last fall a big raccoon got into our apartment through an open window. It was two in the morning. Aretha barked like a maniac and we all ran to see what was wrong.

The raccoon was in the kitchen, examining a piece of Aretha's dog chow. He held it in his little hands proudly, like he'd discovered a big brown diamond. He was not even a tiny bit afraid of us.

He nibbled his diamond carefully. He seemed glad we'd joined him for dinner.

Aretha leaped onto the couch. She was barking so loud I thought my ears would fall off.

Robin ran to get her baby buggy in case the raccoon wanted to go for a ride. My mom called 911 to report a home invasion.

My dad, who only had on his sock monkey pajama bottoms, turned on his electric guitar and made this earsplitting screechy sound to scare off the raccoon.

"Don't you dare go near that animal," my mom warned Robin. She pointed to her cell phone and shushed us. "Yes, Officer, yes. 68 Quiet Moon. Apartment 132. No, he's not attacking anyone. He's eating dog food. Dog chow, actually. Not the wet kind. Kids, stay away. He could be rabid."

"He's not a rabbit, Mommy," Robin said as she wheeled her baby buggy in circles around the living room. "I'm pretty sure he's a beaver."

For a while I just watched them all go crazy. It was kind of entertaining.

Finally I whistled.

I have a really good whistle for a kid. I use my pinkie fingers.

Everyone stopped and stared. Even the raccoon.

"Guys, just sit on the couch," I said. "I've got this."

I walked to the front door and opened it.

That's all I did. Just opened it.

Fog drifted. Frogs chatted. The waiting world was calm.

Everyone sat on the couch. I kept Aretha quiet with her squirrel chew toy. It was covered with dog slobber.

We watched the raccoon finish his food. When he was done, he waddled past us like he owned the place and headed for the open door. He glanced over his shoulder before he left. I could almost hear him muttering *Next time I go to a different place. This family is nuts.*

Lately, I felt like I always had to be on alert for the next raccoon invasion.

33

Saturday morning, I woke up, went into the living room, and found a big empty spot where our TV had been. The room looked naked without it.

My dad was making breakfast. Pancakes and bacon. We hadn't had pancakes and bacon in a really long time.

Robin was sitting at the kitchen table. Aretha was drooling, and Robin's chin was gooey with syrup. "Daddy made my pancakes shaped like Rs. For Robin."

"Do you have a letter preference?" my dad asked me.

He was using his cane, which meant he wasn't feeling great. "You okay?" I asked.

"The cane?" He shrugged. "Just a little insurance policy."

I hugged him. "Plain old circle pancakes would be great," I said. "Where's Mom?"

"Picked up an extra breakfast shift at Toast."

"Daddy sold the TV to Marisol," Robin said. She jutted out her lower lip to make sure we knew she wasn't happy.

"Marisol?" I repeated.

"I saw her dad while I was taking out the trash," my dad said as he poured perfect circles of batter into a pan. "We were talking about the game today, and how his TV had conked out, and one thing led to another. He had the cash, I had the TV, and the rest is history."

"But how are you and I going to watch the game?" I asked.

"We're going to Best Buy it."

I grabbed a strip of bacon. "What's that mean?"

My dad adjusted the heat on the stove. "You'll see. Where there's a will, there's a way."

"Aretha liked watching *Curious George*," said Robin. She set down her plate and Aretha licked it clean.

"You may be interested to hear that Curious George began his existence as a character in a book," said my dad as he flipped a pancake. "In any case, this family needs to spend more quality time together. You know—play cards, maybe. Or Monopoly."

"I like Chutes and Ladders," said Robin.

"Me too." My dad tossed a little chunk of bacon to Aretha. "Too much TV rots your brain."

"You love TV," I said while I started loading the dishwasher.

"That's because TV's already rotted it. There's still hope for you two."

It didn't take long for my breakfast to be ready. "Nice work on the pancakes," I said.

"Thanks. I do have a certain flair." My dad

pointed his spatula at me. "I saw Marisol when Carlos and I were carrying in the TV. She said to remind you about the Gouchers' dachshunds."

"Yeah, we're walking them tomorrow."

"Are dachshunds wiener dogs?" Robin asked.

"Yes, ma'am." My dad nodded. "You know, Jacks, I haven't seen much of Dawan or Ryan or anybody else lately. What's up with that?"

"I dunno. Dawan and Ryan are doing soccer camp. Everybody does different stuff in the summer."

My dad put some dishes in the sink. His back was turned to me. "I'm really sorry about soccer camp, Jacks. Just couldn't swing it."

"No biggie," I said quickly. "I'm kind of growing out of soccer."

"Yeah," my dad said softly. "That happens."

I stared at the sweet steam spinning from my pancakes. I tried hard not to think about Marisol watching our TV, feeling sorry for us while we played Chutes and Ladders and ate bran cereal out of a T-ball cap.

Then I tried not to be annoyed at myself for worrying about something so unimportant.

I grabbed my fork and knife and sliced up my pancakes.

"Whoa," said my dad. "Ease up, Zorro."

I looked up, confused. "Who's Zorro?"

"Masked guy. Good with swords." My dad pointed to my plate. "You were getting a little carried away with the slice-and-dice action."

I looked down at my pancakes. It was true. I'd destroyed them pretty well. But that wasn't what got my attention.

In the middle of the plate, surrounded by maple-syrup mush, were slices of pancake, neatly forming eight letters: *C - R - E - N - S - H - A - W.*

Maybe it was my imagination. Maybe not. In any case, I scarfed them down before anyone could notice.

34

After my mom came home, my dad and I headed for Best Buy. We stopped at the bank, and while my dad stood in line, I grabbed two free suckers, one for me and one for Robin. I always pick purple. If there are no purples, reds are pretty good.

I am not a big fan of yellows.

We were lucky to live in Northern California, I figured. It's really beautiful, except for when there are wildfires or mudslides or earthquakes. Even better, it's a great place to find free food, if you know where to look. The farmers' market at the Civic Center parking lot is a great spot because they give you samples, things like honey in a straw or peanut brittle. Grocery stores are good too, the ones where they have free cantaloupe pieces on a toothpick. Our local hardware store gives away little bags of popcorn on Saturdays, so that's an option, if you get there early enough.

If you're hungry, you wouldn't want to live in Alaska, I'll bet. They probably don't have outdoor farmers' markets very often. Although in Alaska they do have grizzly bears. I would very much enjoy meeting one of those guys.

From a nice, safe distance. A grizzly bear's front claws can be four inches long.

Around here, it's easier to be hungry in winter than in summer. Most people wouldn't expect that, but during the school year you can get free breakfast and lunch and sometimes after-school snacks. Last year they stopped having summer school because there wasn't enough money. So that means no breakfast or lunch when school's out.

They do have free food at the community center food pantry, but that's pretty far away. My dad doesn't like to go there. He says he doesn't want to take food from people who really need it. But I think maybe he doesn't like to go because everyone in line looks so tired and sad.

After the bank, we went to Best Buy, which is this giant store filled with TVs and computers and cell phones and things.

There were two long rows of TVs. Some were huge, taller than Robin, and every one of them was set to the same channel. I guess there are a lot of Giants fans working at that store.

When Matt Cain pitched a curveball, twenty balls flew across twenty screens. One TV sky was a deeper blue. One TV field was a softer green. But the movements were all the same. It was like being in a house of mirrors at the county fair.

Lots of people paused to watch the game with us.

The clerks watched too, when they could get away with it. When one of them asked my dad if he had any questions about the TVs, he said we were just looking.

During the fourth inning, something weird happened. Extremely weird. On everybody else's TV, there were two announcers sitting in a booth. They were wearing black headphones, and they were pretty psyched about a triple play.

On my TV there were two announcers sitting in a booth. They had black headphones and they were excited too.

But on my TV, one of the announcers was a cat. A big cat.

"Crenshaw," I said under my breath.

He was looking right at me. He waved his paw.

I looked at my dad's TV. I looked at all the other TVs.

None of their announcers were giant cats.

"Dad." I sort of whisper-gulped the word.

"Did you see that play?" he asked. "Amazing."

"I saw."

I saw something else, too. Crenshaw was holding up two fingers, making rabbit ears behind the other announcer's head.

Weird, I thought, a cat having fingers. I'd forgotten Crenshaw had them.

Weird, I thought, me worrying about *that*.

"You didn't happen to see a cat just now, did you?" I asked in a casual voice.

"Cat?" my dad repeated. "You mean on the field or something?"

"The cat standing on his head," I said. Because that's what Crenshaw was doing. A headstand on the desk. He was good at it too.

My dad grinned. "The cat standing on his head," he repeated. He looked at my TV. "Right."

"Just messing with you," I said. My voice was trembling a little. "I, uh . . . I changed the channel. That new Friskies commercial was on."

My dad ruffled my hair. He looked at me. *Really* looked, in that way only parents can do.

161

"You feeling okay, buddy?" he asked. "I know things have been a little crazy lately."

You have no idea, I thought.

I smiled an extra-big fake smile that I use on my parents sometimes. "Totally," I said.

The Giants won, 6 to 3.

35

When the game was over, we drove to Pet Food Express. All the way there I thought about Crenshaw.

There's always a logical explanation, I told myself. Always.

Maybe I'd dozed off for a minute and dreamed him up.

Or maybe—just maybe—I was going completely bonkers.

My dad was tired from standing so long at Best

Buy, so I said I'd go get Aretha's dog food. "Smallest, cheapest bag," my dad reminded me.

"Smallest and cheapest." I nodded.

It was cool and quiet inside. I walked past shelf after shelf of dog food. Some contained turkey and cranberries. Some had salmon or tuna or buffalo for dogs who were allergic to chicken. They even had dog food made with kangaroo meat.

Near the food, I saw a rack of dog sweaters. They said things like HOT DOG and I'M A GREAT CATCH. Next to them were sparkly pet collars and harnesses. Aretha would never be caught dead in one of those, I thought. Pets don't care about sparkles. What a waste of money.

I passed a display of dog cookies shaped like bones and cats and squirrels. They looked better than some human cookies. And then, I don't know why, my hand started moving. It grabbed one of those stupid cookies.

The cookie was shaped like a cat.

Next thing I knew, that cookie was in my pocket.

Down the aisle, a clerk in a red vest was on his hands and knees in front of the dog toys. He was wiping up dog pee while a customer's poodle puppy licked his face.

"Collars are half off," the clerk called to me.

I kind of froze. Then I said I was just looking. I wondered if he'd seen me take the cookie. It didn't sound like it. But I couldn't be sure.

"You know, scientists found that dogs maybe really do laugh," I said. My words were spilling fast, like pennies from a holey pocket. "They make this noise when they're playing. It's not exactly panting. More like a puffing sound, sort of. But they think it could be dog laughter."

"No kidding," the clerk said. He sounded grumpy. Maybe because the puppy had just peed on his shoe.

The puppy scrambled over to nose me. He was dragging a boy who looked about four years old. The boy was wearing dinosaur slippers. His nose was running big-time.

"He's wagging," the boy said. "He likes you."

"I read somewhere that when a dog's tail wags to his right, it means he's feeling happy about something," I said. "Left, not so much."

The clerk stood. He was holding the wad of paper towel in his outstretched hand like it was nuclear waste.

I made myself meet his eyes. I felt hot and shaky. "Where's the dog chow? The stuff in the red bag with green stripes?" I asked.

"Aisle nine."

"You know lots about dogs," the little boy said to me.

"I'm going to be an animal scientist," I told him. "I have to know lots."

"I have a sore throat but it's not strep," the boy said, wiping his nose with the back of his hand. "My mom is buying food for King Kong. That's our guinea pig."

"Good name."

"And this is Turbo."

"Also a good name."

I reached into my pocket and felt the cookie there.

My eyes burned and blurred. I sniffled.

"You have a cold too?" the boy asked.

"Something like that." I let Turbo lick my hand and headed to the back.

"He's wagging to the right, I think," the boy called.

36

I'd never stolen anything before last spring. Except for the unfortunate incident with the yo-yo when I was five and used very bad judgment.

It was a surprise how good I was at it.

It's like when you discover you have an unusual talent. Being able to lick your elbow, for instance. Or wiggle your ears.

I felt like a magician. Now you see it, now you don't. Watch Magic Jackson make this quarter appear from behind your ear! Watch this bubble gum disappear before your eyes!

Gum is harder than you'd think. It's the perfect size for slipping into your pocket. But it's usually right next to the place where you pay. So it's easier for a clerk to see you are up to no good.

I'd only shoplifted four times. Twice to get food for Robin, and once to get gum for me.

And now the dog cookie.

I got my start with jars of baby food. Even though she was five, Robin liked eating it sometimes. The stinky meat kind, not even the fruit goo.

Don't ask me why. I will never understand that girl.

We'd stopped at a Safeway grocery store because Robin had to go to the bathroom. She wanted to get something to eat, but my mom said wait till later. While they went to find the restroom, I wandered down the aisles to kill time.

And then I saw the Gerber baby food. I slipped

two jars of chicken and rice into my pockets. Smooth and easy as could be.

Nobody seemed to notice. Probably because who would think a kid my age would steal something that looks like brown snot?

In the next aisle, I passed a guy from my school with his dad. Paul something. He was pushing their shopping cart. They had a giant snack pack of barbecue potato chips and those lemonade drinks in little boxes and a giant bag of red apples.

I waved very casually. An it's-not-like-I'm-showing-bad-judgment-or-anything kind of wave. Paul waved back.

I walked right out the door with Robin and my mom, no sweat. No lightning came down to zap me. No police cars zoomed in with sirens howling like coyotes.

Later at home, I pretended to find the jars in the back of a cupboard. My mom was really happy, and so was Robin.

I was amazed how easy the lying came. It was like turning on a faucet. The words just rushed right out.

I felt guilty for not feeling guilty. I mean, I'd shoplifted. I'd taken something that didn't belong to me. I was a criminal.

But I told myself that in nature it's survival of the fittest. Eat or be eaten. Kill or be killed.

They say those things a lot in nature films. Right after the lion eats the zebra.

Of course I wasn't a lion. I was a person who knew right from wrong. And stealing was wrong.

But here's the truth. I felt crummy about the stealing. But I felt even worse about the lying.

If you like facts the way I do, try lying sometime. It'll surprise you how hard it is to do.

Still and all. Even though I felt lousy, I had fixed a problem.

Robin gobbled down the chicken-and-rice goo so fast that she threw up most of it on my book about cheetahs. I figured maybe that was my punishment.

37

When we got home from the pet store, I went to my room, half expecting to see Crenshaw lounging on my bed. Instead, I found Aretha. Her nose was buried in my keepsakes bag, and she had a guilty expression on her face. She for sure had something in her mouth, but I couldn't see what it was.

"Show me," I said. I pulled the stolen dog cookie from my pocket. It was a little mushed on one side. I held it out so that Aretha would drop whatever was in her mouth and snatch the cookie. But she wasn't interested.

Probably she didn't want to eat stolen goods.

Aretha slunk toward my bedroom door, tail dragging, and I saw what she was holding. It was the clay statue I'd made of Crenshaw, clutched between her teeth.

"You don't want that old thing," I said, but she seemed to disagree. As soon as she was out of my bedroom, she galloped down the hall and scratched urgently at the front door.

"Want me to open it, baby?" Robin asked. She turned the knob and Aretha rocketed outside.

"Aretha! Stop!" I yelled. Usually she waited by the door for me, flopping her tail hopefully. Not today.

I grabbed her leash. She was heading straight for Marisol's house, which was about half a block down the street. Aretha loved Marisol. She also loved Marisol's seven cats, who enjoyed sunbathing on the screened-in back porch.

I found Aretha in Marisol's old sandbox. Marisol

didn't use it anymore, but Aretha loved it. She was already digging a hole. Sand fanned skyward like sprinkler spray.

Aretha was an expert digger. She'd buried two water bowls, a TV remote control, a pizza box, a ziplock bag of Legos, three Frisbees, and two of my homework folders there. Not that my teachers had believed me.

Marisol was wearing flip-flops and her pajamas, which had snoring sheep on them. She loved pajamas. In first grade, she wore them to school every day until the principal told her she was setting a bad example.

In her left hand, Marisol had a large saw. Her hair was covered with sawdust. She almost always smelled like fresh-cut wood.

Marisol loved to build things, especially things for animals and birds and reptiles. She made birdhouses and bat shelters. Dog carriers and cat trees. Hamster habitats and ferret houses.

At the end of her fenced yard were planks, a sawhorse, and a big circular saw. A small house-looking thing was on the ground, half built. It was for one of her cats.

"Hey," I said.

"Hey," she said. "You ready for the yard sale?"

"I guess."

"Aretha brought me that," Marisol said. She pointed to my Crenshaw statue, which was sitting on the picnic table. "Dropped it right at my feet."

"I made it when I was little," I said with a shrug. "It's lame."

"If you made it, it's not lame," Marisol said. She put down her saw and examined the statue.

Aretha stopped digging and looked up at us hopefully. Her face was covered in sand. Her tongue lolled sideways.

"It's a cat," Marisol said, brushing off a piece of grass stuck to the bottom. "A standing cat with a baseball cap. I like it. I like it very much."

I shrugged, hands in my pockets.

"Was this for the yard sale?" Marisol asked. "How much is it?"

"It's not for sale. Aretha got into a bag of my stuff is all."

"I have three dollars."

"For that?" I laughed. "It's just, you know. A hunk of clay. Some school project."

"I like it. It's . . . intriguing." Marisol reached into her pajama pocket. She handed me a wad of money that looked like it had been through the laundry.

"Keep it," I said. "Think of it as a going-away present."

Her eyes went wide. "What are you talking about, Jackson? You're not—"

I waved a hand. "No. It's probably nothing. My parents are just being their usual weird selves."

It wasn't the truth, not completely. But it wasn't not the truth.

"You'd better not move. I'd miss you too much. Who would help me with See Spot Walk? And anyway, I love your weird parents."

I didn't respond.

"We've got the dachshunds tomorrow," Marisol said.

"Yep." I pointed to the miniature zigzag staircase she was building. "Where's that going?"

"Antonio's old room, when he heads off to college this fall. Or maybe Luis's. His room is just full of boxes."

"You're like an only child," I said.

"It's kind of boring," Marisol said, pushing a strand of hair behind her ear. "There's no one to fight with. It's too quiet."

"Sounds nice."

"I like your apartment. There's always something going on. Sometimes it's just me and Paula for days on end." She rolled her eyes.

Marisol's dad was a salesman and her mom was a pilot. They traveled a lot, so Paula, an older woman, often stayed with Marisol. Marisol refused to call her a "nanny" or "babysitter" or "caregiver." She was just "Paula."

Marisol grabbed a tape measure to check the

height of the staircase she was making. "I'm going to attach this staircase to the wall, see? Like so? And then put shelves way up high for the cats to climb to. It'll be cat paradise."

"Speaking of cats . . ." I bent down to fill in the hole Aretha had made. The sand was soft and dry. "Did I ever tell you . . ." I hesitated, then pushed on. "Did I ever tell you that I had an imaginary friend when I was little?"

"Really? Me too. Her name was Whoops. She had red hair and was extremely naughty. I blamed her for everything. Who was yours?"

"He was a cat. A big cat. I don't remember much about him."

"You should never forget your imaginary friend."

"How come?"

"What if you need him someday?" Marisol reached for a piece of wood. "I remember everything about Whoops. She liked to eat brussels sprouts."

"Why?" I pretended to gag.

"Probably because I like brussels sprouts."

"You never told me that. I may have to reconsider our friendship."

"Because of Whoops? Or the brussels sprouts?" She yanked a nail out of a plank with her hammer. "Hey, new bat fact. In Austin, Texas, they have the world's largest urban bat colony. Like a million and a half of them. When they fly out at night, you can see them on the airport radar screens."

"Very cool," I said. "Ms. Malone would love seeing that."

Marisol and I both had Ms. Malone for fourth grade. She taught all subjects, but she loved science best of all. Biology especially.

We chatted about bats while we watched Aretha dig another hole. Finally I said, "Well. Gotta go."

I hooked Aretha to her leash. She licked my cheek with a sand-covered tongue. It felt like a cat's.

"Did Whoops ever . . . you know?" I made myself ask the question. "Did she ever come back after you outgrew her?"

Marisol didn't answer right away. Sometimes she

just let a question sit for a while, like she needed some time to get acquainted with it.

"I wish she *would* come back," Marisol said, gazing at me. "I think you'd like her."

I nodded. "Yeah. I guess I could overlook the brussels sprouts thing."

"Jackson?"

"Yep?"

"You're not really moving, are you?"

I studied her question the way she'd studied mine. "Probably not," I said, because it was easy, and easy was all I could manage.

Aretha and I were almost to the front yard when Marisol called, "It needs a name."

"You mean the statue?"

"Yeah. Something unique."

"What do you want its name to be?" I asked.

She didn't answer right away. She took her time.

Finally she said, "Crenshaw would be a good name for a cat, I think."

38

I crossed the street. Twice I looked back. Marisol waved.

Crenshaw.

It must have been written on the bottom of the statue. By my teacher or my mom or me.

There's always a logical explanation, I told myself. Always.

39

That night I sat on my mattress, staring at what was left of my bedroom. My old bed, shaped like a red race car, the one I'd outgrown ages ago, was in pieces. A sticker on the headboard said $25 OR BEST OFFER. Dents in the carpeting hinted at what used to be there. A cube where my nightstand should have been. A rectangle where my dresser once stood.

My mom and dad came in after Robin was asleep.

"How you doing, bud?" my dad asked. "Definitely roomier, huh?"

"It's like camping out," I said.

"Without the mosquitoes," said my mom. She handed me a plastic mug of water. I kept it by my bed in case I got thirsty in the middle of the night. She'd been doing that for as long as I could remember. The mug, which had a faded picture of Thomas the Tank Engine on it, was probably nearly as old as I was.

My dad touched the mattress with his cane. "Next bed, let's make it more serious."

"Not a race car." My mom nodded.

"Maybe a Volvo," said my dad.

"How about just a bed bed?" I asked.

"Absolutely." My mom leaned over and combed her fingers through my hair. "A bed bed."

"We'll probably make some bucks at the sale," my dad said. "So there's that."

"They're just things," my mom said quietly. "We can always get new things."

"It's okay. I like all the space," I said. "I think

Aretha does, too. And Robin can practice batting without knocking anything over."

Both my parents smiled. For a few moments, neither spoke.

"All right, we're outta here," my mom finally said.

As he turned to leave, my dad said, "You know, you're such a big help, Jackson. You never complain, and you're always ready to pitch in. We really appreciate that."

My mom blew me a kiss. "He's pretty amazing," she agreed. She winked at my dad. "Let's keep him around."

They closed the door. I had one lamp left. Its light carved a yellow frown on my carpet.

I closed my eyes. I imagined our things spread out on the lawn tomorrow. My mom was right, of course. They were just things. Bits of plastic and wood and cardboard and steel. Bunches of atoms.

I knew all too well that there were people in the world who didn't have Monopoly games or race car beds. I had a roof over my head. I had food most of the time. I had clothes and blankets and a dog and a family.

Still, I felt twisted inside. Like I'd swallowed a knotted-up rope.

It wasn't about losing my stuff.

Well, okay. Maybe that was a little part of it.

It wasn't about feeling different from other kids.

Well, okay. Maybe that was part of it too.

What bothered me most, though, was that I couldn't fix anything. I couldn't control anything. It was like driving a bumper car without a steering wheel. I kept getting slammed, and I just had to sit there and hold on tight.

Bam. Were we going to have enough to eat tomorrow? *Bam.* Were we going to be able to pay the rent? *Bam.* Would I go to the same school in the fall?

Bam. Would it happen again?

I took deep breaths. In, out. In, out. My fists clenched and unclenched. I tried not to think about Crenshaw on the TV or the dog cookie I'd stolen.

Then, just the way I'd taken that cookie, without understanding why, without thinking about the consequences, without any *reason*, I grabbed my mug and hurled it against the wall.

Bam. It splintered into shards of cracked plastic. I liked the noise it made.

I waited for my parents to return, to ask what's wrong, to yell at me for breaking something, but no one came.

Water trickled down the wall, slowly fading like an old map of a faraway river.

40

I woke in the night, sweaty and startled. I'd been having a dream. Something about a giant talking cat with a bubble beard.

Oh.

Aretha, who likes to share my pillow when she can get away with it, was drooling onto the pillowcase. Her feet were dream-twitching. I wondered if she was dreaming about Crenshaw. She'd certainly seemed to like him.

Wait. I felt my brain screech to a halt, like a cartoon character about to careen off a cliff.

Aretha had *seen* Crenshaw.

At the very least, she'd reacted to him. She'd tried to lick him. She'd tried to play with him. She'd seemed to know he was there.

Dogs have amazing senses. They can tell when a person is about to have a seizure. They can hear sounds when we hear only silence. They can unearth a piece of hot dog buried at the bottom of a neighbor's trash can.

But however amazing dogs can be, they cannot see somebody's imaginary friend. They cannot jump into their owner's brain.

So did that mean Crenshaw was real? Or was Aretha just responding to my body language? Could she tell I was freaking out? Or did she figure I'd come up with a brand-new game called Let's Play with the Giant Invisible Cat?

I tried to recall how she'd acted back when we

were living in our minivan. Had she sensed Crenshaw's presence then?

I couldn't remember. I didn't want to remember.

I covered my face with my drooly pillow and tried to go back to sleep.

41

"Ribbit," said something.

I opened my eyes. A frog was on my forehead.

He looked familiar. Like the windowsill visitor Crenshaw had wanted to eat.

I turned my head and the frog leaped off. Next to me lay a human-sized cat. On top of Crenshaw lay a medium-sized dog. And on top of Aretha sat the frog.

Two of the three were snoring.

I sat up on my elbows. I blinked. Blinked again.

I'd left the window ajar. That explained the frog. It did not explain the cat.

"You're back," I said.

"Morning," Crenshaw murmured, his eyes still closed. He wrapped his paws around Aretha, snuggling close.

"Just tell me this," I said. I crawled off my mattress and stretched. "How do I get rid of you for good?"

"I'm here to help you," Crenshaw said. He yawned. His teeth were like little knives. He pulled one of Aretha's velvety ears over his eyes to block out the sun.

"What did you mean about telling the truth?" I asked.

"Truth is important to you," said Crenshaw. "So it's important to me. Now, please allow me to continue my slumber."

"Are you my conscience?" I asked.

"That depends. Would you like me to be?"

I checked my closet, just in case there was a giant invisible possum or gopher or something lurking there. "No," I said. "I'm managing just fine on my own."

"Oh, really?" said Crenshaw. "What's that abominable dog treat lying on the floor?"

The cookie. Aretha still hadn't eaten it.

I tossed it out my window. Maybe squirrels wouldn't mind eating something stolen.

"Remember when you stole the yo-yo back when you were five?" Crenshaw asked.

"When my parents caught me, I tried to blame you."

"Everyone always blames the imaginary friend."

"Then my parents made me take it back and apologize to the store."

"I think you see where this is going." Another yawn. "Now, if you don't mind, I'll be taking a little catnap."

I stared at him. He'd made me feel mystified and annoyed and more than a little crazy. And now he was making me feel guilty. One way or another, I had to get him out of my life.

"By the way," I said before leaving the room, "you're hugging a dog."

I didn't see what happened next, but I heard a hiss and a yowl. Aretha dashed past me at high speed.

She hid under the kitchen table for an hour.

42

Selling your stuff at a yard sale is a weird experience. It's like walking around with your clothes on inside out. Underwear on top of jeans, socks on top of sneakers.

The insides of your apartment are spread out for everybody to see and touch. Strangers finger the lamp that used to be on your bedside table. Sweaty guys sit in your dad's favorite chair. Little stickers are on everything. Five dollars for your old tricycle that still has sparklers on the wheels. Fifty cents for the Candy Land game.

It was a sunny Sunday morning. Lots of neighbors were selling stuff, too. It almost felt like a party. My mom sat at a card table with a little box to hold money. My dad walked around while people bargained with him and said how about two dollars instead of three.

When he got too tired to walk, he sat in a folding chair and played songs on his guitar and sang. Sometimes my mom would sing harmony.

My main job was to carry stuff to people's cars and to keep an eye on Robin. She was pulling someone's old wagon that had a $4 sign taped to it. In the wagon was her trash can with the blue bunnies, which my parents had promised she could keep.

It wasn't so bad, watching our things get sold. I told myself that every dollar we made was a good thing and that it was all just meaningless stuff. And it was nice to be with our neighbors and friends, drinking lemonade and talking and singing along with my parents.

Around noon, we'd sold almost everything. I

watched my mom count up the money we'd made. She looked over at my dad and shook her head. "Not even close to what we need," she said quietly.

Before he could respond, a skinny man with a ponytail approached my dad. He pulled out a fancy leather wallet and asked my dad if his guitar was for sale. My dad and mom exchanged a glance. "Could be, I suppose," said my dad.

"I have one that's for sale, too," my mom added quickly. "It's back in the apartment."

My dad held up his guitar. Sunlight darted off its smooth black body. "It's a beauty," said my dad. "Lotta history."

"Dad," I exclaimed, "you can't sell your guitar."

"There's always another guitar around the bend, Jacks," said my dad, but he wouldn't meet my eyes.

Robin ran over. She was still towing the wagon, which nobody had bought. "You can't sell that!" she cried. "It's named after Jackson!"

"Actually," I said, "*I* was named after the guitar."

"It doesn't matter!" Robin's eyes welled with tears.

"That's a keepsake for keeping. Here. You can have my trash can for free, mister. Instead."

She thrust her trash can into the skinny man's hands. "I, uh—" the man began. "I . . . it's a dynamite trash can, sweetie. I really like the . . . the bunnies. But I'm more in the market for a guitar."

"No guitars, no way," Robin said.

My dad gave the man a helpless shrug. "Sorry, man," he said. "You heard the lady. Tell you what, though. Why don't you give me your phone number? In case we have a change of heart. I'll walk you out to your car."

Together, my dad and the man headed toward a sleek black car. My dad's left foot dragged a little. Sometimes that happens with MS.

They exchanged scraps of paper, talked, and nodded. The skinny man drove off, and I had a feeling that my dad's change of heart had already happened.

43

About an hour later, our landlord came by our apartment. He had an envelope in his hand. He hugged my mom and shook my dad's hand and said he wished things could be different. I knew what the paper was because I could see the words at the top.

It said FINAL EVICTION NOTICE. Which meant we had to leave the apartment.

My dad leaned against the wall. There wasn't anywhere to sit anymore.

"Kids," he said, "looks like we're going to be taking a little drive."

"To Grandma's?" asked Robin.

"Not exactly," said my mom. She slammed a cupboard door shut.

My dad knelt down next to Robin. He had to use his cane to keep steady. "We have to move, baby. But it will be fun. You'll see."

Robin's eyes bored into me. "You told me it would be okay, Jacks," she said. "You lied."

"I didn't lie," I lied.

"This isn't Jackson's fault, Robin," my mom said. "Don't blame him. Blame us."

I didn't wait to hear any more. I ran to my room. Crenshaw was lying on my bed.

I sat next to him, and when I buried my head in his fur, he didn't object. He purred loudly.

I cried a little, but not much. There wasn't any point.

Once I read a book called *Why Cats Purr and Other Feline Mysteries.*

Turns out nobody knows for sure why cats purr.

It's surprising how much stuff adults don't know.

44

At four that afternoon, Marisol came to the door. She was wearing flip-flops and flowered pajamas. She had the Gouchers' dachshunds, Frank and Beans, with her. "Did you forget?" she asked. "You were supposed to meet me."

I apologized and took Frank's leash. As we started down the sidewalk, I was surprised to see Crenshaw walking ahead of us. Not as surprised as I might have been a day or two ago. But still. There he was, gliding along on his hind legs, doing the occasional cartwheel or handstand.

I didn't know how to tell Marisol why we were leaving. I'd never told her about our money problems, although she may have guessed by the way I didn't offer her anything to eat when she came over, or by the way my clothes were always a little too small.

I wasn't lying, exactly. It was more that I left out certain facts and focused on others.

I didn't want to do it, of course. I liked facts. And so did Marisol. But sometimes facts were just too hard to share.

I decided to tell Marisol something about a sick relative, about how we had to go take care of him, and how it was an all-of-a-sudden kind of thing. But just as I started to speak, Crenshaw leaned close and whispered in my ear: "The truth, Jackson."

I squeezed my eyes shut and counted to ten. Slowly.

Ten seconds seemed like the right amount of time for me to stop being crazy.

I opened my eyes. Marisol was smiling at me.

And then I told her everything. I told her about how worried I'd been and how we were hungry sometimes and how afraid I was about what might come next.

We walked toward the school playground. Crenshaw strode ahead and rocketed down the tube slide. When he got to the bottom, he looked at me and nodded approvingly.

And then, I don't know why, I told Marisol one more fact.

I told her about Crenshaw.

45

I waited for her to tell me I was nuts.

"Look." Marisol knelt down to scratch Beans behind the ear. "We don't know everything. I don't know why my brothers feel the need to burp the alphabet. I don't know why I like to build things. I don't know why there are no rainbow M&M's. Why do you have to understand everything, Jackson? I like not knowing everything. It makes things more interesting."

"Science is about facts. Life is about facts. Crenshaw is not a fact." I shrugged. "If you understand how something happens, then you can make it happen again. Or not happen."

"You want Crenshaw to go away?"

"Yes," I said loudly. Then, more softly: "No. I don't know."

She smiled. "I wish I could see him."

"Black. White. Hairy," I said. "Extremely tall."

"What's he doing right now?"

"One-handed push-ups."

"You're kidding me. I'd love to see that."

I groaned. "Look, it's okay. Go ahead and call a psychiatrist. Have me committed."

Marisol punched me in the shoulder. Hard.

"Ow!" I cried. "Hey!"

"You're annoying me," she said. "Look, if I were worried about you, I'd tell you so. I'm your friend. But I don't think you're going crazy."

"You think it's normal to have a giant kitty taking bubble baths in your house?"

Marisol puckered her lips like she'd just chewed a lemon. "Remember in second grade when that magician came to the school fair?"

"He was so lame."

"Remember how you went behind the stage and figured out how he was making that rabbit appear? And then you told everybody?"

I grinned. "Figured it right out."

"But you took the magic away, Jackson. I liked thinking that little gray bunny appeared in a man's hat. I liked believing it was magic."

"But it wasn't. He had a hole in the hat, and—"

Marisol covered her ears. "I didn't care!" she cried, punching me again. "And I still don't care!"

"Ow," I said. "Again."

"Jackson," Marisol said, "just enjoy the magic while you can, okay?"

I didn't answer. We walked in silence, following our usual route. Past the little park with the fountain. Past the bike path I'd ridden a zillion times, back when I had a bike. Past the place where I broke my arm popping a wheelie. Past the sign that said WELCOME TO SWANLAKE VILLAGE.

"I read that swans stay together for life," Marisol said.

"Usually," I said. "Not always."

"You and I will be friends for life," Marisol said. She stated it like any nature fact. Like she'd just said "The grass is green."

"I don't even know where my family's going."

"Doesn't matter. You can send me postcards. You can e-mail me from the library. You'll find a way."

I kicked at a stone. "I'm glad I told you about Crenshaw," I said. "Thank you for not laughing."

"I can practically see him," said Marisol. "He's doing backflips on my front lawn."

"Actually, he's doing the splits on your driveway."

"I said *practically* see him." She smiled at me. "Fun fact, Jackson. You can't see sound waves, but you can hear music."

46

That evening, Crenshaw and I went out to the backyard.

Crenshaw liked night.

He liked the way the stars took their time showing up. He liked the way the grass let go of the sun's warmth. He liked the way crickets changed the music.

But mostly he liked to eat the crickets.

We lay there, me on my back, Crenshaw on his side, with Aretha nearby gnawing on a tennis ball.

Every so often she looked up, ears cocked, sniffing the air.

It felt good, talking as the night took over. It almost made me forget that we were leaving the next day. It almost made me stop feeling the anger and sadness weighing me down like invisible anchors.

Crenshaw trapped a cricket under his big paw.

I told him crickets were considered lucky in China.

"Crickets are considered delicious in Thailand," he replied. His tail looped and snaked like a lasso at a rodeo. "And in cat-land."

I chewed on a piece of grass. It's a good way to distract yourself when you're hungry. "How do you know that?"

Crenshaw glanced at me. "I know everything you know. That's how imaginary friends operate."

"Do you know things I don't know?"

"Well, I know what it's like to be an imaginary friend." Crenshaw slapped at a moth with his other front paw. The moth fluttered over his head like it was laughing at him.

"I hate moths," he said. "They're butterfly poseurs."

"I don't know what that means."

"Butterfly wannabes."

"If you know everything I know, how come you know words I don't know?"

"It's been three years, Jackson. A cat can do a lot of learning in that time. I read the dictionary four times last month."

He tried for the moth again and missed.

"You used to be faster," I pointed out.

"I used to be smaller." Crenshaw licked his paw.

"I've been meaning to ask you why you're so much bigger. You weren't this big when I was seven."

"You need a bigger friend now," said Crenshaw.

My mom walked by with a box of clothing to put in the minivan. "Jackson?" she said. "You okay?"

"Yep."

"I thought I heard you talking to somebody."

I cast a look at Crenshaw. "Just talking to myself. You know."

My mom smiled. "An excellent conversational partner."

"Do you need any help, Mom?"

"Nope. Not much to pack, when you get right down to it. Thanks, sweetie."

Crenshaw lifted his paw. The cricket scrambled for freedom. Down went the paw. Not enough to kill the poor bug. Just enough to annoy him.

"Do you ever feel guilty about the way cats torture things? Bugs, mice, flies?" I asked. "I know it's instinct and all. But still."

"Of course not. It's what we do. It's hunting practice. Survival of the fittest." He lifted his paw, and this time the cricket made a quick getaway. "Life isn't always fair, Jackson."

"Yeah," I said, sighing. "I know."

"In any case, you're the one who made me a cat."

"I don't remember deciding that. You just sort of . . . happened."

Aretha dropped her ball in front of Crenshaw. He sniffed it disdainfully.

"Cats do not play," Crenshaw told her. "We do not frolic. We do not gambol. We nap, we kill, and we eat."

Aretha wagged wildly, still hopeful.

"Fine." Crenshaw blew on the tennis ball. It rolled a few inches. Aretha nabbed it with her teeth and tossed it in the air.

"That was playful of you," I said. I plucked a new piece of grass to chew on. "For someone who doesn't play."

"I fear you may have made me with a hint of dog thrown in." Crenshaw shuddered. "Sometimes I actually want to . . . to roll in something stinky. A dead skunk maybe, or some ripe trash."

"Dogs do that because—"

"I know why. Because they're idiots. I also know you will never, ever catch this fine feline specimen stooping so low."

I sat up. The moon was thin and yellow. "Anything else I put in the mix?"

"Well, I sometimes worry I have a bit of fish in me. I rather like water."

219

I thought back to my first-grade self. "I liked fish a lot when I was seven. I had a goldfish named George."

"Of course," said Crenshaw. "You liked a lot of animals back then. Rats, manatees, cheetahs. You name it." He groaned. "Bats, too. No wonder I like to eat mosquitoes."

"Sorry," I said, but I couldn't help smiling.

"At least you worked with animals. I have a friend—nice guy—who was made entirely of ice cream. Hated hot weather."

"Wait." I let that sink in. "You mean you know *other* imaginary friends?"

"Of course. Cats are solitary, but we're not completely antisocial." He yawned. "I've met Marisol's imaginary friend, Whoops. And your dad's."

"My dad had an imaginary friend?" I cried.

"It's more common than you might think, Jackson." Crenshaw yawned again. "I feel a snooze coming on."

"Wait," I said. "Before you go to sleep, just tell me about my dad's friend."

Crenshaw closed his eyes. "He plays the guitar, I think."

"My dad?"

"No. His friend. Plays the trombone, too, if I recall correctly. He's a dog. Scrawny. Not much to look at."

"What's his name?"

"Starts with an *F*. Unusual name. Franco? Fiji?" Crenshaw snapped his fingers. Which is not something cats generally do. "Finian!" he said. "It's Finian. Nice guy, for a dog."

"Finian," I repeated. "Hmm. Where are you, Crenshaw, when you're not with me?"

"You've seen a teachers' lounge, right?"

"I've peeked. We're not allowed in. Mostly I saw a lot of coffee cups and Mr. Destephano napping on a couch."

"Picture a giant teachers' lounge. Lots of people

waiting and snoozing and telling stories about exasperating, amazing children. That's where I stay. That's where I wait, just in case you need me."

"That's all you do?"

"That's plenty. Imaginary friends are like books. We're created, we're enjoyed, we're dog-eared and creased, and then we're tucked away until we're needed again."

Crenshaw rolled onto his back and closed his eyes. A good cat fact to know is that they only expose their tummies when they feel safe.

His purr filled the air like a lawn mower.

47

I couldn't fall asleep that night. Sounds echoed off the walls of our empty apartment. Shadows loomed and shrank. A question kept nagging at me: Why did things have to be this way?

Life isn't always fair, Crenshaw had said. His words reminded me of an interesting nature fact Ms. Malone had taught us last year in fourth grade.

Bats, she said, actually share food with each other. She was talking about vampire bats, the ones that slice open sleeping mammals in the dark of night. They don't actually suck blood. It's more like they lap it up, which is awesome enough. But the really amazing part, the *no way* part, is that when they get back to their caves, they share with the unlucky bats who haven't found anything to eat. They actually puke up warm blood into the hungry bats' mouths.

If that's not the coolest nature fact ever, I don't know what is.

Ms. Malone said maybe bats are altruists, which means they're sharing to help the other bats, even if it's a risk. She said some scientists say yes, some say no.

Scientists love to disagree about things.

Ms. Malone looked at me then, because even though it was only like the third week of school, she already had me pegged pretty well. "Jackson," she said, "maybe you'll be the one to settle the great *Are Bats Nice Guys?* debate."

I said probably not, because I wanted to be a

cheetah or manatee or dog scientist, but I would keep bats in mind as a backup plan.

Ms. Malone said something else about bats that day.

She said she sometimes wondered if maybe bats are better human beings than human beings are.

48

I must have finally fallen asleep, because I woke from a horrible nightmare. I was panting. Tears streamed down my cheeks. The moon was wrapped in fog.

Crenshaw placed a paw on my shoulder. Gently he butted his head against mine.

"Bad dream?" he asked.

"I don't remember it, really. I was in a cave, I

think, and I was yelling for someone to help me, and nobody would listen."

"I'll help," said Crenshaw. "I'll listen."

I turned to him. Looking in his eyes, I could see myself reflected.

"I can't go with my family," I said. My own words surprised me. "I can't live in the minivan again. I don't want to have to worry anymore. I'm tired, Crenshaw."

"I know," he said. "I know."

I blinked. The answer was obvious.

I had to run away.

It wasn't going to be much of a trip. I'd just have to ask Marisol if I could stay with her. She had plenty of room. I could help around the house.

I leaped up. Crenshaw watched me, but he didn't say a word.

It wasn't like I had a lot to pack. I grabbed my pillow, my keepsakes bag, some clothes, and my toothbrush.

The way I figured it, I'd go over to Marisol's house

before my family woke up. Marisol was an early riser. She wouldn't mind.

It was hard to find a piece of paper and a pencil, but I managed. Aretha and Crenshaw watched me chew on the pencil as I tried to decide what to write.

"What should I say?" I asked, as much to myself as to Crenshaw.

"Tell the truth to the person who matters most," said Crenshaw. "You."

And so I did.

Dear Mom and Dad,

Here are the facts.
I am tired of not knowing what is going to happen.
I am old enough to understand things.
I hate living this way.
I'm going to live with Marisol for a while.
When you figure things out, maybe I can join you.

Love,
Jackson

PS: Aretha likes to sleep on a pillow, so don't forget.

PPS: Robin needs to know what's happening, too.

In an envelope, I put ten dollars I'd made from walking the Gouchers' dachshunds. On the outside I wrote: To cover two unfortunate incidents where I used very bad judgment, please give $7 to Safeway (for 2 jars of Gerber chicken and rice) and $3 to Pet Food Express (for a cookie shaped like a cat).

49

Ta-tap-ta-ta-tap.

It was Robin, knocking at my door. "Jacks?"

I dropped my pencil. "Go to sleep, Robin. It's late."

"It's scary in my room."

"It'll be morning soon," I said.

"I'll just wait here by your door," Robin said. "I have Spot to keep me company."

I looked at Crenshaw. He held up his paws. "Don't

ask me. Human children are infinitely more complicated than kittens."

"Please go back to bed, Robin," I pleaded.

"I don't mind waiting," she said.

I stood.

I went to the door.

I hesitated.

I opened it.

Robin came in. She had Spot, her pillow, and her
Lyle book.

I looked at her.

I looked at my note.

I crumpled it up and tossed it aside.

We read Lyle together until we both fell asleep.

50

When I awoke, Robin, Aretha, and Crenshaw were spread out on my mattress. Robin and Aretha were both drooling a little.

Sitting on the floor across from us were my mom and dad. They had on their bathrobes. My dad had my crumpled note, flattened out, in his lap.

"Good morning," my mom whispered.

I didn't answer her. I didn't even look at her.

"Fact," my dad said softly. "Parents make mistakes."

"A lot," my mom added.

"Fact," said my dad. "Parents try not to burden their kids with grown-up problems. But sometimes that's hard to do."

Robin stirred, but she didn't wake.

"Well, it's hard being a kid, too," I said. I was glad I sounded so angry. "It's hard not to know what's happening."

"I know," said my dad.

"I don't want to go back to that time," I said, my voice getting louder with each word. "I hated you for putting us through it. It wasn't fair. Other kids don't have to sleep in their car. Other kids aren't hungry."

I knew that wasn't true. I knew that lots of other kids had it worse than I did. But I didn't care.

"Why can't you just be like other parents?" I demanded. I was crying hard. I gasped for breath. "Why does it have to be this way?"

My mom came over and tried to hug me. I wouldn't let her.

"We're so sorry, sweetheart," she whispered.

My dad sniffed. He cleared his throat.

I looked over at Crenshaw. He was awake, watching me carefully.

I took a deep, shuddery breath. "I know you're sorry. But that doesn't change the way things are."

"You're right," said my dad.

No one talked for a few minutes. The only sound was Crenshaw, purring gently. And only I could hear him.

Slowly, very slowly, I began to feel my anger changing into something softer.

"It's okay," I finally said. "It's really okay. I just want you to tell me the truth from now on. That's all."

"That's fair," my dad said.

"More than fair," my mom agreed.

"I'm getting older," I said. "I can handle it."

"Well, then here's another fact," said my dad. "Last night I called the guy who wanted to buy our guitars. He told me his brother owns that music store down by the mall. He needs an assistant manager. His brother also has a garage apartment behind the store that won't be occupied for a month. It'd give us a roof over our heads for a little while, anyway. Maybe some more work."

"That's good, right?" I asked.

"It's good," my dad said. "But it's not a certainty. Here's the thing, Jackson. Life is messy. It's complicated. It would be nice if life were always like this." He drew an imaginary line that kept going up and up. "But life is actually a lot more like this." He made a jiggly line that went up and down like a mountain range. "You just have to keep trying."

"What's that expression?" asked my mom. "Fall down seven times, get up eight?"

"More fortune cookie wisdom," said my dad. "But it's true."

My mom patted my back. "Starting today, we'll

be as honest with you as we can. Is that what you want?"

I looked over at Crenshaw. He nodded.

"Yes," I said. "That's what I want."

"All right, then," said my dad. "It's a deal."

"Fact," said my mom. "I'd really like some breakfast. Let's go see what we can do about that."

51

The music store looked pretty run-down. We waited in the car while my parents went to talk to the owner. It took a long time. Robin and I played cerealball with her T-ball cap and some sugarless bubble gum.

"You remember those purple jelly beans?" Robin asked.

"The magic ones?"

Robin nodded. "They were maybe not so magic."

I sat up straighter. "What do you mean?"

"They were from Kylie's birthday party." Robin pulled on her ponytail. "I just wanted you to think they were magic. But there's no such thing. Of course."

"I don't know," I said. "Could be magic happens sometimes."

"Really?" Robin asked.

"Really," I said.

When my parents came out of the store, they were smiling. They shook a man's hand, and he gave my dad a set of keys.

"Got the job," my dad said. "It's part-time, but with everything else, it should help. And we can stay in that apartment for a month, anyway. Hopefully by then we'll have come up with yet another plan. We really want to keep you and Robin at the same school. We're going to do our best, but there are no guarantees."

"I know," I said, and even though it didn't solve all our problems, I felt a little better.

The garage apartment was tiny, with only one bedroom. There was no TV, and the carpeting was a weary beige.

Still. It had a roof and a door and a family who needed it.

52

The article I read about imaginary friends said they often appear during times of stress. It said that as kids mature, they tend to outgrow their pretend world.

But Crenshaw told me something else.

He said imaginary friends never leave. He said they were on call. Just waiting, in case they were needed.

I said that sounded like a lot of waiting around, and he said he didn't mind. It was his job.

The first night in our new apartment, I slept on a chair in the living room. I woke up in the middle of the night. Everyone else was sleeping soundly.

As I headed to the bathroom to get a drink, I was surprised when I heard the water running. I knocked, and when no one answered, I opened the door a crack.

Bubbles floated and danced. Steam billowed. But through the mist I could make out Crenshaw in the shower, fashioning a bubble beard.

"Do you have any purple jelly beans?" he asked.

Before I could answer, I felt my dad's hand on my shoulder. "Jackson? You okay?"

I turned and hugged him hard. "I love you," I said. "And that's a fact."

"I love you, too," he whispered.

I smiled, recalling the question I'd been meaning to ask. "Dad," I said, "have you ever known anyone by the name of Finian?"

"Did you say *Finian*?" he asked with a faraway look in his eyes.

I closed the bathroom door, and as I did, I caught another glimpse of Crenshaw. He was standing on his head. His tail was covered with bubbles.

I squeezed my eyes shut and counted to ten. Slowly.

Ten seconds seemed like the right amount of time for me to be sure he wasn't going to leave.

When I opened my eyes, Crenshaw was still there.

There had to be a logical explanation.

There's always a logical explanation.

Meantime, I was going to enjoy the magic while I could.

ACKNOWLEDGMENTS

My heartfelt thanks to

- The Feiwel and Friends pantheon: Rich Deas, Liz Dresner, Nicole Moulaison, and Mary Van Akin for their patience and breathtaking talents; Liz Szabla for her TLC, remarkable insights, and gracious good humor; Angus Killick for his leadership and enthusiasm; and Jean Feiwel for just about everything;

- Elena Giovinazzo, agent extraordinaire, at Pippin Properties, Inc., for her guidance and friendship;
- Artist Erwin Madrid for bringing Crenshaw to life;
- The amazing students and staff of the Monarch School in San Diego, California, a unique campus for students affected by homelessness, for sharing their stories;
- My friends and family for pretending not to notice my long chats with an imaginary cat;
- Jake and Julia for tolerating the "don't bug me while I'm writing unless you're bleeding" mandate;
- and Michael, for asking to borrow that can opener so many years ago.

Thank you for reading this FEIWEL AND FRIENDS book.

The friends who made

Crenshaw

possible are:

JEAN FEIWEL, Publisher

LIZ SZABLA, Editor in Chief

RICH DEAS, Senior Creative Director

HOLLY WEST, Associate Editor

DAVE BARRETT, Executive Managing Editor

NICOLE LIEBOWITZ MOULAISON, Senior Production Manager

ANNA ROBERTO, Associate Editor

CHRISTINE BARCELLONA, Associate Editor

EMILY SETTLE, Administrative Assistant

ANNA POON, Editorial Assistant

Follow us on Facebook or visit us online at mackids.com.

OUR BOOKS ARE FRIENDS FOR LIFE.